IN THE PRESENCE
OF GODS

A Baseball Fairy Tale

Rob Murphy

Rob Murphy

REMIII

ISBN-13: 9781234567890
ISBN-10: 1477123456

Cover design by: Art Painter
Library of Congress Control Number: 2018675309
Printed in the United States of America

Inspired by and dedicated to Richard Short

Special thanks to Michael Short for his wisdom and guidance

CONTENTS

INTRODUCTION

On July 9, 1976, my Uncle and I sat talking on his backyard deck on a beautiful summer day in Michigan. We had just finished watching a Tigers game on the TV that featured a young man named Mark "The Bird" Fidrych. He had pitched another gem and Fidrych had become a national sensation over the course of that summer. He played the game with the enthusiasm of a little boy. Fidrych talked to the baseball before he threw every pitch and then celebrated each play with the enthusiasm of a true fanatic, and, for that one magical summer, he threw the ball like Cy Young.

Fans, in turn, couldn't get enough of this strange Bird, and on that day in July pitching in front of a packed house at Tiger Stadium, Fidrych gave up only one run in nine innings. Despite his brilliant performance, the Tigers lost to the Royals 1-0. But the loss didn't matter to the fans in the stadium because they were so captivated and excited by the way that he played baseball that they refused to leave the stadium until The Bird came back out and made a curtain call. Mark "The Bird" Fidrych won the hearts and minds of Detroit that summer and brought enormous pride, joy, and excitement to the area.

As we talked on the deck, my Uncle struggled to articulate the improbability of the fairy tale that Mark "The Bird" Fidrych was living. The crux of his disbelief was how was it possible for a

complete unknown to do the things that he did during the summer of 1976.

In his search to verbalize the implausibility of the Bird's accomplishments, my Uncle said that the only thing more improbable would be a fairy tale about someone like himself becoming a major league star. At the time, my Uncle was 40 years old, and in no way athletic or capable of playing major league baseball.

Fairy Tales are stories about the young and beautiful getting what they want, but the seed of his idea stuck with me and simmered on low heat for the last 40 years. So why not a fairy tale about a middle age, out of shape, everyman doing the impossible. How would that work, and what would that look like? This story is my version of that scenario.

IN THE PRESENCE OF GODS

A Basball Fairy Tale

Rob Murphy

THE YARD

Amber light spilled through canopies of green, and shadows shifted as a soft breath of wind gently moved above. By mid-June, it had not yet rained, and this day would be dry as well. By 10 a.m., it was eighty degrees, and the earth gave out that stagnant smell of dirt that happens on hot, windless mornings in Michigan.

The dad watched as the boy moved out to start his morning routine. He would go from place to place, checking in on all the little landmarks of the yard that he found interesting. A particular hole, a scratch on the fence, a loose board on the shed, or even just an odd divot in the grass were all worthy of his consideration. In some places, he would explore a long time, and others stop for a second or two. It had become their habit that when it was time to play, the boy would squat down to his knees and pick at the ground and wait for his dad.

The dad never understood what the boy did when he kneeled, but he knew that if he interrupted or joined him too soon, the boy would become upset and run back inside, and the cycle would have to start again. So, the dad made a point of letting him have his time before joining him in the yard. On this morning, the boy settled near the oak on the right. That meant today would be Wiffle ball.

The black-haired boy was skinny, tall, strong, and athletic, with not an ounce of fat on him. He tied the laces on his red high-tops extremely tight and insisted on knee-length tube socks. He paired his black silky sports shorts with the same yellow T-shirt at all times of the year during all weather conditions: sun, rain, snow. In truth, he always wore at least three pairs of shorts and six to ten T-shirts all at the same time. Each article was carefully chosen and put on in a specific order, and this padding made him look much bigger or at least thicker than he was.

The backyard was a large rectangle that had become an oasis of protection and wonderment for the boy, and he knew every inch of it. Near the house on each side were several large oaks that arched out to shade the house and frame the yard.

Between the oaks was a well-worn porch with three much newer but very ugly steps leading to the lawn. The flowers were in full bloom by now, and the vegetables were starting to reach a size worth noticing. A dusty, pecky cedar fence outlined the yard. The ashy old boards were tall, but given all the holes in the wood, it was hardly private.

Directly across from the house, in one corner, at the back, in what served as the dead center field for Wiffle ball games was a large, faded shiplap shed placed precisely to the edge of the lot line. The fence continued on each side of the shed, and sun-fed vines grew gracefully on its surface.

It was the boy's habit to end his morning exploration by going to that part of the yard that he used to communicate which game he wanted to play on that day. If he knelt at oak on the left, it meant they would play golf, and if at the swing set, it said the frisbee was needed. They would play a game of football if he stopped at the shed door, and the rotten piece of carpet in front of the oak tree on the right meant today they would be playing Wiffle ball. Actually, for quite a while now, all they played was Wiffle ball.

This ratty old carpet was roughly the size and shape of a home plate because that was its original intent. But now it stayed where it was because the boy liked to lift the rug and study the explosion of tunnels and paths cut by bugs under the protection of the fragile fabric. Each time he looked at the landscape under the carpet, it had changed, a new insect, beetle, or worm had moved in.

He would study this world for a while and then, as if taking a test, he would carefully draw shapes or lines in the dirt between the spaces in the dead, wispy blades of grass. He would follow those same lines again and again, then stop and stare for a very long time before doing it again. Sometimes he would watch ants marching among the blades, and their mysterious paths had a hypnotic effect on him, and he would watch fixated as they went about their business. When finished, he would place the carpet gently back in its exact place before considering it for a while, as well.

On this particular day, the boy focused on the tiny beads of sweat that had slowly formed on his arm in the morning sun. Eventually, they would grow, gather, and run in small rivers down his arm, bouncing off little hairs, changing directions, then moving on, always down, shifting haltingly between the strands like ants between blades of grass.

The dad always wondered what the boy was thinking but knew he could never understand. Suddenly, the boy stood up, then slowly tilted his head to one side and looked to the leaves fluttering above; at his waist, his hand ceased its endless flipping. Beyond that, he stood still, entirely still, for several minutes, watching the sparkles of green and yellow now dancing across his face. The dad knew that when the boy stood back up, it signaled an end of the routine and meant it was time for the dad to go outside. Today was Wiffle ball, and that told the dad to bring the long yellow plastic bat and an odd white plastic ball.

The boy was autistic and a mute; he made no sounds, ever. While he was extremely attentive to everything happening around him, his interactions with others were often just a small head tilt to the side or a change of speed in the way his hand flicked. He never made eye contact; his gaze was to just to the side of a face, never in the eye. A noticeable change of expression was rare and happened only during an exhilarating moment in a backyard game.

The boy could offer physical expression through mimicry of his favorite TV memories. When excited, he would copy Major League gestures and actions like Gibson's home-run chug and Fisk's fair-ball wave, but his favorites were the full-blown out or safe call of a dynamic Major League umpire on a close play.

He had a fantastic ability to mimic the batting stances of big-league players and favored the oddest and most distinct stances. He could perfectly reproduce the painful-looking closed and twisted batting stance of John Wockenfuss, or the one used by Jeff Bagwell, with the insanely wide leg spread. He was dead on with Tony Batista's impossible to use wide-open stance and batted quite well using Willy Horton's exaggerated posture, in which he held his bat as high as possible over his head. He had memorized dozens of stances, and every time he batted, after every out or hit, a new batting stance would appear. If he ever used a personal batting stance, it remained hidden among the parade of imitations of the legends he loved.

When they played Wiffle ball, the boy always batted first. They had played for several years, and each knew the rules and what to expect. As pitchers, both had outlandish curves, drops, and knucklers, and they could hit anything that didn't break the way the pitcher intended. In this yard, they were the masters of the game.

The rules of their particular game of Wiffle ball were simple. If the ball hit the face of the shed or fence in the air, it was a double. If it landed on the shed's roof, a triple, and anything over the wall was a home run. There were three outs, and anything hit fair that wasn't a double, triple, or home run was an out. Three strikes were an out; four balls were a walk. If the pitcher hit the tree with the ball, it was a strike, and the cartoon *tonk* sound it made turned the tree into a great umpire. They played with six Wiffle balls at a time, so they didn't have to chase, scores were low, innings were quick, games were five inning long and they always played three games per session.

The habit was to play three games back to back, and the dad would narrate the action a la Ernie Harwell when the boy was winning—which lately meant always! All young boys like to win, and for the most part, this boy never lost. There was a time when the dad would be sneaky and play poorly so the boy could make a miraculous comeback, but those days had long since passed as the boy's skills were now far beyond those of the father.

Over the several years that they had been playing, they had become excellent players. Each had full command of bat and ball, as well as the variety of ways the ball could be pitched and hit. It was problematic when others wanted to play as their shorthand was absolute, and novice players just interrupted the flow, annoying everybody. Friends and family had long since learned to watch and enjoy the game by never trying to play with them.

Both dad and boy were excellent pitchers, so most games were less than ten runs total. The thick, hard white plastic of a Wiffle ball flew wonderfully when hit just right, but hitting it was very difficult with the thin yellow bat.

Wiffle balls are very close in size to a regular baseball, but thick, white plastic is used to make them. One hemisphere is completely solid, while the other side of the ball is full of evenly spaced holes. There is a kind of magic in the way that air flows around the holes in a Wiffle ball that allows a talented pitcher to generate outrageous curves, rises, and drops. The boy, in particular, had become masterful at manipulating the holes of the ball so that when he threw it, it would curve two to three feet, if not more.

Each Wiffle ball pitcher does it a little different, but the basics are as follows: If the pitcher grips the ball and keeps the holes on the top of the ball, it will fly mostly straight but will drop. If they grab the ball with the holes near their thumb, it will curve to the left. Hold the ball with the holes to the finger side of their hand, the ball will bend to the right. All these actions can be decreased or increased by using different speeds and arm angles. Both dad and boy threw wicked fast, so curves were nasty and mean, resulting in games that seldom totaled ten runs.

It took the boy about forty-five minutes to win two out of three games and then, as if flipped by a switch, he was done playing Wiffle ball. It was the boy's turn to drink cold water from the garden hose when the dad asked if he wanted to see a Mud Hens game that day. Instantly the boy dropped the garden hose and went inside the house. That was his signal for yes.

THE STADIUM

The drive to Fifth Third Field that night was short and straightforward. The dad and the boy would travel to three or four games per summer. By professional standards, it was a small stadium of about ten thousand seats situated near a couple of big convention centers in Toledo, Ohio. This game was a night game, and the dad thought there was something magical about watching a baseball game played under the lights.

The stadium is called Fifth Third Field, and it was home to the Toledo Mud Hens, an International League team and the Triple-A affiliate of the Detroit Tigers. The dad hated the idea of naming stadiums after banks or other corporations as it felt cheap and sleazy, at least to him. As a kid, going to Tiger Stadium was a religious event, and the stadium itself was a holy place. When they replaced Tiger Stadium with Comerica Park, it felt as if they painted a cross on the side of a cinder-block building and called it the Vatican. It was just wrong.

However, Fifth Third Field was clean and comfortable, and compared to the heavy corporate feel of Comerica Park, it was a great place to watch a game, especially for the boy, with all his issues. It had become the venue of choice when the pair wanted to see a game. The fresh night air was a welcome relief from the heat of the day. They found their seats as the game was starting, serenaded to the announcements of tonight's promotional event.

They always got seats in about the same place along the first-base line, as repetition and familiarity made things easier

8

for the boy. Repetitive actions were essential for him, and so they always did things the same way when they went to the ballpark. They always ate a hot dog, and the boy insisted that his hot dog have mustard, and he would only drink a Sprite. Their meal happened in the third inning, followed by the bathroom break during the fourth. As had become their routine, the boy watched the game intently but seldom reacted to what he saw.

The dad made a point to quietly explain what was happening into his ear, and the boy for his part leaned in a tiny bit to listen. By now, it was clear to the dad that the boy knew the game quite well and understood most of the smaller details that made it enjoyable. Over time, the boy had developed an uncanny knack of predicting pitches that each pitcher was about to throw. He would watch the first inning closely, and by the second was predicting sliders and fastballs and curves with amazing accuracy.

It took the dad a very long time to understand what the boy was doing, but before each pitch, the boy would hold his hand out slightly in front of him and make one of two unique flicking motions. When the pitch was going to be a fastball, he would open all his fingers like someone flicking water. To indicate a breaking ball, he waved his fingers downward like someone testing the temperature of a bathtub. The boy had always flapped his hand, so at first, the dad just assumed these ballpark-only hand flips were just part of that. Once the dad figured out the boy's system of communication, he was stunned by how accurate it was. The dad watched intently, searching to understand what the boy was seeing, but had so far been unable to solve the puzzle.

But tonight, would be unusual for other reasons. Baseball has a long history of special events and giveaways at the ballpark going back decades. In the old days "Bat Day" was always an essential event at Tiger Stadium, and large crowds would show up and each kid was given a free baseball bat as a prize for attendance. Most teams have days where they give away a bat, ball, cap, or helmet, and at most parks they are well attended. Typically, each kid of a certain age would get one of these items as a prize for coming to the game.

Some teams, in a desperate attempt to lure fans, have gotten a bit unusual over the years. The Tampa Bay Rays have always had a hard time drawing fans to Tropicana Field, so they have offered some bizarre promotions. They once gave away Carlos Peña toothbrush holders, of all things. The Yankees gave away flower seeds. As odd as that might seem, the weirdest of all time was the Chicago White Sox' "Disco Demolition Night." On this night, fans got in for free if they brought a disco record. A riot erupted at the ballpark on that night back in 1979, when the White Sox put those records in a pile in the middle of the field and blew them up. Tonight's promotion was unusual, but in the grand scheme of things, it was pretty safe by comparison.

On this night at Fifth Third Field, the team announced that they were having a promotion they called "Bat Night." Other teams gave away a free baseball bat; in contrast, the Mud Hens' version was to give away an opportunity to bat against live pitching from a professional pitcher. The team would give $5,000 to any fan that could hit a home run over the fence off one of the Mud Hens professional pitchers. On this night, the pitcher was the team's star reliever, whom everyone expected to be called up to the majors any day. The Mud Hens had been doing "Bat Night" for a couple of years, and it had become a fan favorite, although a fan had yet to hit a foul ball, much less a home run.

As the vendor handed the dad the two hot dogs, a Sprite, and an eight-dollar beer, the loudspeaker came to life: "Tonight's Bat Night raffle winner is ticket number 5-8-8-5. Please check your ticket to the ballpark for the winning number. The holder of the winning ticket should report to the box office be-hind home plate."

As the dad and boy settled in with their food, they be-came lost in the dad's narration and didn't pay attention to the announcement. After a while, a young man behind the dad tapped him on the shoulder, and the dad looked up at him.

"Hey, man, you didn't check your ticket, are you gonna check your ticket?"

"Oh, OK!" said the dad.

With that, the dad fished in his pocket for their tickets to the game. Hot dog in one hand, beer in the other, he found his tickets and held them up to the young man. "What were the numbers?"

The young man greedily snatched them and read the numbers looking closely at each ticket. "5-8-8-6, close but not this—one. Let's see 5-8-8-5! Oh my God! Oh my God! You won, you won!"

With that, the young man and his friends started jumping, frantically gesturing, pointing at the dad and his boy. Everybody around them went crazy, slapping him on the back and making general chaos. Security guards and ushers appeared and brought them through a series of dark hallways until they found themselves in a fluorescent office under the stands behind home plate.

An administrator appeared in a Mud Hens blazer. He wore a fake smile and carried a clipboard and talked at breakneck speed in a well-rehearsed spiel, leaving no time for answers as he plowed through his list of rules.

"Congratulations—what's your name?"

But before the dad could speak his name, Blazer Dude said, "Follow me."

Then he turned and led them down the stairs toward wherever it was they needed to go. As they walked, he talked. "OK, these are the rules: at the end of this inning, we will give you a helmet, a bat, and one of our guys will pitch to you. The umpire will call balls and strikes just like a real at bat. You will get three strikes or four balls, and at that time, the at bat ends. If you hit a ball fair and it's not a home run, then you're out, and the at bat ends. It's all or nothing, home run or nothing, and the at bat ends—to win, you have to hit a home run. If you hit a home run, it has to be fair and over the fence in the air—no bounce overs. If you hit a home run, you must run the bases and touch them all to claim the prize. However, before we let you try, you need to sign a disclaimer absolving the Mud Hens organization of all blame if you get hurt or killed. Will you sign the disclaimer?"

With that, Blazer Dude abruptly stopped and looked at the dad, waiting for an answer.

It startled the dad how fast the man spoke. He was taken aback by the pace of it all.

"Sure, I guess so. . . Listen, my boy is autistic. I can't leave him alone, can he come out there with me?"

"How old is he? If he is less than eighteen, then he will have to wait in the stands—no, your boy doesn't look eighteen, so he can't go on the field!"

Blazer Dude abruptly disappeared down a hallway and walked through a door. The dad realized they were quite lost in this hidden, dingy space underneath the stands, and had been left alone. Thinking he wasn't going to be allowed to bat, the dad led the boy back down the hall, trying to find his way back to the stands.

Almost as suddenly as he had left, Blazer Dude reappeared, jogging toward them, yelling, "Wait, where are you going?" He was out of breath. "So, this is what we decided—the boy can go too, but he has to wear a helmet. We're gonna pull out a screen for him to stand behind, so there's no way he can get hit, but he has to wait behind the screen—will that work?"

"I think so."

"Great! Sign this here, champ . . . and here . . . and here . . . here . . . write next of kin . . . and an emergency contact phone number."

The dad quickly signed without reading, and just as suddenly Blazer Dude blurted: "OK, the inning just ended, let's go!" He took clipboard from the dad's hands.

"Follow me, champ."

He led them like a whirlwind blowing past a bathroom, down the hall, through a locker room, up a ramp, and finally to a gate. Blazer Dude opened it, and suddenly the trio were walking into the surreal world of a professional baseball field between innings of a real a game.

As they moved onto the field, a screen was moved past the dad and up near home plate. He heard his name announced as the winner of today's raffle and as this night's hitter, and the crowd cheered respectfully but mainly ignored what is happening. Someone handed the dad an old bat and a beat-up batting helmet and instructed them to follow. The dad was still carrying his beer but set it down to put on the batting helmet, then picked it up again. The batting helmet was missing the ear pads, so it was way too loose even for his big head and hung low enough to rub against his glasses. Someone then handed him another helmet and said, "Put it on him—hurry up."

He held the helmet in front of his son's face so he could see it. "So I'm gonna get to do this, but do you think you can wear this helmet for me, just like me? Can you do that?" The boy didn't move away when the dad slowly tried to put it on him. The boy held very still, and the helmet slid on. The dad carefully studied the boy, looking for signs that the boy was OK with the feel of the batting helmet. "Can I have a high five?" he asked, holding his hand up. The boy did not respond. "OK, then."

With that, he gently moved the boy behind the screen. "Can you wait here while I try to do this? Can you stay behind this screen for me? It will only take a minute, OK?"

The boy's hand flicked at an increased rate that told the dad he understood and was OK with all this. The dad picked up his beer and moved toward the batter's box, still looking at the boy.

At no point in his life was the dad considered athletic, although he was a huge sports fan. In the last ten years, the only real form of exercise he got was playing in the yard with the boy, and he did that almost every day. The dad was 5'9", not strong, and was physically less than average in every other regard. He was very good at drinking beer, though, and at age forty suffered from allergies and was at least fifty pounds overweight.

Most of the time, he sported some of a sort of baseball cap, as he had an extensive collection of them. Under his hat was an enormous, mostly bald head. The hair that was left was pathetic, and it was thin and in desperate need of cutting. He wore large, thick, wire-frame glasses that allowed him to see quite well, but without them, the world was fuzzy. Like his head, his eyes were huge and rather bulgy, giving the impression to those first meeting him that they might pop out of his head at any minute. He was also extraordinarily bowlegged and that, combined with his bunions, meant that his gait had the look of a much older man.

He always dressed casually, wearing a selection of cargo shorts and one of his million logoed T-Shirts. He typically paired that with a never buttoned bowling shirt that he used to hide armpit sweat. The dad was a person of prodigious sweat, and golf and bowling buddies marveled at his ability to soak through everything with minimal effort. He did not own dress shoes, and although he did not have diabetes, it was his habit to either wear diabetic sneakers with white socks, or flip-flops. Today, he wore his lime-green flip-flops with no socks.

While the dad was a huge baseball fan, the only version of the sport he ever played was Wiffle ball, no Little League, high school, nothing. He was never even invited to play softball with his buddies at work, so he had no expectations of success today.

He was near the batter's box when the umpire yelled, "Play Ball!" The dad looked at him as he waddled into place, bat in one hand, beer in the other. "Time!"

The umpire had noticed the beer and stepped out from behind the catcher. "Buddy, you need to get rid of the beer."

The dad looked startled. He held out the beer toward the catcher and said, "Can you hold my beer?"

"Are you serious? No, dude!" The catcher chuckled from behind his mask.

So, the dad stepped over the plate and set down the beer in the other batter's box. As he rose up from that, he could see the boy looking at him. The few fans that were watching started to laugh a bit as the catcher jumped up, picked up the beer, moved it farther away from home plate, and set it down a couple of feet in front of the screen.

"Take a practice swing, buddy," the catcher said, smiling as he returned to his position behind the plate. "He is only gonna throw what I tell him, and I'm gonna tell him to just throw fastballs for ya—fastballs are easy, so relax, have fun!"

The only batting stance the dad knew was the one he used for Wiffle ball, and it was odd; actually, it was very bizarre. His extreme bow leggedness meant that when he bent his knees, they also pushed very wide apart, like a ballerina in the *plié* position. He kept his elbows so close together they almost touched, then leaned back toward the umpire a bit and tilted his bat away from the pitcher like Rod Carew used to do. It was goofy, but it worked for him. Before this moment, he just never tried it with a real baseball bat.

The dad stepped into the batter's box again and got in his stance and took that practice swing the catcher told him to, but it caused his too-big helmet to fall off, which, of course, knocked off his glasses. At this, the crowd has started to notice the pathetic participant and began to heckle him. Up to this moment, he hadn't been aware of the people in the stands. He became quite self-conscious, now in a panic as he tried to retrieve his glasses.

"Come on, buddy, get it together we got a game to play here. Hurry up," said the ump. "Playball!" He gestured to the pitcher to throw the ball.

The dad still wasn't entirely done putting himself back together when the first pitch came in with a loud pop. "Streeeerike Ooone!" boomed the umpire from behind the plate.

"Wait, I wasn't ready," he thought to himself, angered that he was still getting his glasses in place when the ball came in. The collective crowd that was now paying attention didn't like this quick pitch and started yelling at the umpire.

Thwack! "Streeerike 2!" boomed again from behind the

plate. Another quick pitch, and the dad had not seen either one of them.

He had watched a million games on TV and knew the game well, so instinct took over. He stepped out of the batter's box and loudly called time, holding up his hand to the umpire like a real big leaguer. "Time," said the ump quietly. Angered by these quick pitches, he flashed the umpire his best pissed-off look.

The catcher chuckled, "C'mon buddy."

The umpire added, "Let's get this over with."

In response, the dad calmly crossed the plate, picked up his beer, and took a sip before slowly setting it back down, all the while looking at the ump. The crowd roared with laughter at this and more when he then walked over to the boy and bent low to talk with him.

The excitement, the buzz, the overwhelming crackling of five thousand people all talking at once, screaming, waving, moving—to most people, the stadium was a swirl of chaos that confused and dazzled the senses. However, the boy's normality was in another dimension that allowed him to process all the elements of this chaos as if it were one voice. In spite of outward appearances, the boy was the only one fully aware of what was going on in the stadium that night.

The dad approached, and then his face suddenly swelled many times in size, bent and distorted, as if expanded by the lens of a giant glass, like the world of an M.C. Escher painting. The boy had been studying his dad's actions for the last several minutes, and this allowed him to check carefully on his father's condition. His father was confused and scared, and the boy wanted to calm him and go over everything he had been trying to teach him, but time was not expanding right now. He knew that the dad was a slow learner and didn't listen well, so he decided to focus on reminding him how to hit a baseball. "Maybe it would be enough," he thought.

The dad bent down to the boy, but in truth, he did not have anything to say—this was gamesmanship, and he wanted to show the umpire that he would not allow himself to be bullied. The dad took a long look at the boy, then stood up and took a long, slow walk, circling all the way around behind the umpire before turning back toward the batter's box. Using perfect form, he moved back into the box. He remained looking at the pitcher, back hand extended flat and open to the ump—the universal sign "real" hitters use to maintain timeout while they get ready to hit.

At this, the ump politely waited as the dad put both hands on the bat. "Ready, buddy?" said the umpire in a low voice. The dad gave a little nod with his head still fixed, focused on the pitcher. The umpire pointed at the pitcher, who immediately went into his windup.

The dad heard the ball hit the bat, but it was all so fast he didn't see where it went. The act of swinging knocked his helmet off, and that knocked off his glasses, so he never saw the flight of the ball. The crowd erupted with the loudest sound of the day. He dropped the bat and bent down to retrieve his glasses. He felt the catcher's hand on his back and heard an excited voice say, "Dude! It's gonna go! Dude, you gotta run."

As he put his glasses on, his boy was the first thing he saw. The boy was on his toes and wide eyed, looking directly back at him—right in the eye.

"Buddy, run, you did it! It's gone!" the catcher half yelled, half giggled as he gently shoved the dad and jogged with him to get him moving. This action jarred the dad back to reality, and he started looking around and located first base, where he saw the first-base ump circling his arm in the home-run signal.

He started his odd, bowlegged jog toward first base, looking like a clown in flippers, and the crowd went berserk at the sight of it. As the dad approached the base, he looked back long enough to see the boy and saw his hand flicking at the fastest pace it ever had.

Suddenly he was spread out face down in the red dirt of the infield. His toes stung from the force of hitting first base, and his face and mouth were full of the dirt of Fifth Third Field.

Then he realized his glasses had disappeared again. Aware of the crowd's roar and not wanting to embarrass himself in front of his son, all he could think was to get up as fast as possible. As he rose to his feet, he felt something between his toes—then he felt a sharp pain on his bare foot from the crunch of stepping on his glasses.

He dropped to his hands and knees, now searching the dirt at first base. "Great hit, man! Oh man, you broke your glasses, that sucks," said the first basemen, helping collect the broken parts and putting them in the dad's hands.

By this point, the crowd was going crazy, and he still had three bases to run. "C'mon, run it out now—get going now, c'mon," said the first-base umpire.

At a loss for what to do, the dad held up the now armless eyeglasses to his face. He tried to spit out the remains of that mouth full of dirt. This filthy splurge went just one inch and dribbled down in a huge, disgusting slather on the front of his happy face T-shirt. Defeated and barefoot, he started toward second base, one hand holding glasses to his face while he ran. "Oh man, that's gross," said the first basemen as the dad jogged away.

The dad made it to the second base and rounded toward third. But, his glasses were so dirty that he tried to blow them off. Doing this caused one of the lenses to pop out, and him to trip yet again, much to the delight of the roaring crowd.

Completely humiliated, he got up and chugged on. Then, as if some unseen god were manipulating a puppet, he started mimicking Kurt Gibson's walk-off home run gesture from Game 1 of the 1988 World Series. Seeing this larger than life pumping gesture coming from such a pathetic creature caused the crowd to go absolutely, off-the-charts loud. Rounding third, he could see a big group of players from both teams gathered at home plate waiting to greet him. In the center of this crowd of players, waiting with a big smile and both hands raised to high five him, was the boy.

COMING HOME

The drive home was awful. First of all, he hurt—a lot. Not only had he not tried to run in twenty years, he hadn't fallen for any reason in his adult life. When he tripped over first base, he had fallen hard, without breaking his fall, so everything hurt. Not only was he dirty, old, and beat up, but he could not see correctly either.

When he stepped on his glasses at first base, they broke into four distinct pieces, and while a group of players looked, they never did find the lens he lost at second base. Luckily, he had some duct tape in his trunk and used it to hold the remaining parts of his glasses together. It worked, but driving home on just one lens was tricky.

Making things worse, the flip-flop he wore on the gas pedal side destroyed itself when he tripped over the first base, so it was no longer wearable. He hated driving barefoot and felt lucky to find one of his wife's fluffy winter boots in the trunk of his car. With the zipper undone, he managed to get it on his foot, and while very tight, he preferred that over the feeling of a dirty bare foot on the gas pedal.

Caught near blind without his glasses in the wild celebration at home plate, he managed to step barefoot on his cup of beer, sopping both feet completely. His wet feet were quickly covered in a delicious coating of mud from the red dirt around home plate, and now in the confines of his airtight car, his allergies shifted into high gear. With every cough, sneeze, and itch, that last scratched-up lens would wiggle out of view on him. The drive home was miserable.

He was still quite miserable and still sneezing as he pulled into the driveway. As the car settled to a stop and he shifted the vehicle into the park, the boy jumped out and sprinted into the house. The dad sat in the car for several minutes, hoping to calm his heart before going inside. He closed his swollen, red eyes, and tilted back to rest.

Immediately, his car door swung open, and his wife was talking at him in her concerned voice. "What happened, honey, are you OK? Strange people have been calling all night—I had to unplug the phone. What happened?"

Before he could answer his neighbor appeared in time to interrupt in a loud baritone voice: "That was fantastic, that was the greatest thing I've ever seen. They've played it on every channel—you're even on Sports Center."

"What are you talking about. . . ?" said the wife.

"Is that the check? They gave you a giant check—how cool. Hey, can I see it?" said the neighbor, opening the back door and reaching in for the check. "Wow! Five thousand bucks. That was so fantastic! What are you gonna do with it?" he boomed on.

"Five thousand dollars? For what? What did you do?" whispered the wife.

Before he could answer, the dad wanted out of the car. The dad hurt badly and needed to slowly swing each leg around one at a time to pre-position himself for getting out of the vehicle. Before rising, he looked up at his wife.

She saw before her the epitome of pathetic. She looked down on an odd-looking man with big red eyes, surrounded by a filthy, scratched-up face. The face looked back at her through some odd eyeglass thing, globed up with wads of grotesque, sticky silver tape. Her mind raced as she tried to comprehend what had happened to him. What was that gross stain on his shirt, and why was he wearing one of her boots, and why one flip-flop? "Oh my God, honey, what happened? Did you get beat up?"

The dad got up slowly and started moving up the sidewalk toward the house. As he did, the neighbor told the story.

"He just hit the greatest home run ever. It's all over the TV. He crushed it. I didn't know you were a ballplayer. Look at this. They gave him five thousand dollars."

She held the dad's arm to help him, then whispered, "Honey, what is he talking about?"

With that, the dad stopped and looked deeply into the mom's eyes like an exhausted old dog. "I will tell you about it, but right now, I hurt a lot. I really need to take a shower and lay down."

The neighbor jumped in, interrupting again. "That's OK; it's all over the TV, turn on the TV, you can see right there what he did!" boomed the big baritone.

REALITY

The boy stood outside the open bedroom door for a very long time looking in as his father slept. The boy liked to watch his father sleep and found it comforting. The soft yellow glow that usually surrounded the sleeping man was different today. Ordinarily smooth patterns hung in a cloudy presence around him, but today they danced in staccato, jagged waves, and in a way the boy had never seen before. Something was wrong with his father.

As the dad's eyes opened, things began to hurt. His face throbbed, his knees ached, and his wrists were sore. His great big eyes felt like they were going to explode and stung more with each blink. Even his toes were stiff. Then he moved, and he realized the depth of his pain. "How could one little at bat cause so much pain?" he thought to himself.

He moved to rise, and a sharp pain shot through his back. Finally he reached a sitting position and turned on the bed-side light. He noticed the phone sitting on his night table, then picked it up and pressed a series of buttons. He put it to his ear and realized it wasn't working. He fumbled a bit, found the cord, plugged it back in, and pressed the button again. "Hi—" Instantly, the person on the other end interrupted and started asking questions, leaving him only a chance to say one or two words at a time.

"Yes . . . hey . . . listen . . . no . . . hey . . . let me . . . yes . . . no . . . OK . . . will . . . ." Finally, he just hung up the phone.

He took a slow breath, and as he let it out the phone rang, so he picked it up.

"Yes, it is, who is this?" He held the phone to his ear for several seconds before interrupting. "I'm sorry, I'm not interested." He hung up.

Instantly the phone rang again. Annoyed, the dad closed his eyes, as if to meditate a bit, and took another cleansing breath. He opened his eyes and looked at the phone until the third ring, then picked it up. It was his boss from work. . . .

"Hello. . . . That's OK. . . . No . . . I had to hang—no. . . . No. . . . Yes. . . . Yes. . . . Hey, listen, please let me talk—I was calling to say I'm going to be late; I need to go to the doctor. . . . No, just very sore. . . . A chiropractor. I'll be in after that." He hung up again.

The phone immediately rang. Irked, he unplugged it. It felt like it took him hours to shuffle out to the kitchen. The boy and his mom were already up and eating breakfast. He stopped at the coffee pot first, then joined them, moving very slowly the entire time. "You're moving like you got hit by a truck," said the mom.

"I feel like it. It's unbelievable. I had no idea I was so out of shape."

"I watched the replays on TV. Pretty exciting. Is all this just from that?"

"I'm telling you—I feel like I got hit by a truck, everything hurts. Just chuckling is painful."

Suddenly the boy got up from the table and came over between them and stood silently by the dad's side, looking down toward the cup of coffee.

The boy was troubled by his father's colors and that they were behaving badly that day. He could see the crimson clouds in his father's left hand were especially disruptive, talking with the patterns in his neck and shoulders and causing them to misbehave terribly as well. Colors were very fragile, but the boy decided he must stop this bad behavior. Being careful not to harm, he floated his fingers just above the wine-red cloud blooming from between his dad's thumb and finger. This action bruised them, and the red clouds squealed in pain, angering the patterns who fought with him. But the boy continued floating his fingers and watched the sands of sleep flow until the impish beings snuggled in and gently fell to slumber.

The parents watched as the boy slowly reached out his hand as if to touch the dad's hands with just the tiniest tips of his fingers. But he did not. His fingers stopped and held the smallest breath above his father's skin—the boy stayed in this the position for several seconds. The parents held their breath until the boy withdrew his hand and then stared intently at that spot for several seconds. Then, for no apparent reason, the boy turned and ran outside to the yard.

The mom and dad remained still. Stunned, they looked at each other, not sure what had just happened. Finally, the mom whispered, "He's never done that before!" The dad moved his head gently in agreement, and realizing that his pain was now gone, he watched the boy move out toward the yard.

WORK

The dad worked in a large factory in charge of what workers called the "Tool Cage." He spent his days in this chain-link area surrounded by all manner of contraptions and tools that the workers in a large factory could ever need. Everyone in the building knew him, but he always worked alone. When someone in the factory needed something, they would come to the cage, and he would get it for them. Most of the time, his day was quiet, as he typically had just three or four an hour come to the cage.

The dimensions of the tool cage was about the size of a small gymnasium. The tool cage was still locked when he arrived at 2 p.m. The gate to the enclosure was triple locked and required two keys and a combination padlock to open. The entrance to the tool cage was Dutch door style and allowed him to open the entire thing or just the top half only. When he was in the cage, only the top half was open, and the bottom half remained locked to prevent others from wandering in.

His decades-old office desk was just inside the door to the right. On it, he had a large white calendar with leather corners covered in at least eight years' worth of doodles and scribbles. It was stuck in December of the year it ran out; the dad had never bothered to get a new one. Sitting on the calendar was an old PC, a rotary phone that was even older, and the remains of a dot matrix printer piled high with magazines and old newspapers. Next to the phone, on the left, was his coffee pot, above that were twenty years' worth of clippings and notes randomly plastered on an old corkboard. To the left of the door was a smaller heavy steel table, deeply pitted from the sharp corners of tools slamming into it for the last two decades.

Immediately inside the internal circumference of the fence were heavy steel shelves that grew up from the concrete floor, stopping only at the chain-link ceiling. On the back of each shelf, a thin sheet of steel blocked out all light from coming into the cage. The interior of the enclosure was a low maze lit by fluorescent lights that cast the underside of most shelves into dark shadow. The shelves were packed so close together that the dad could barely move among them without turning sideways.

Tool and die shops make devices called tools and dies. Tool and die making is an art form and only the best of machinists end up working as one. The men and woman who make tool and die components design and make the molds, gages, cutting tools, jigs and fixtures and stamps used in everything that is mass produced. They are also known as die, tool, jig or mold makers. To the untrained eye a perfectly engineered tool and die can in the end look like a weird alien puzzle but they are essential component to making all of the things people use every day. The dad supplied the tool and dies to the tool makers that allowed them to make the latest tool and die.

Most of the shelves in the tool cage were packed with a menagerie of exotic tools and die contraptions devised by people working in the factory. The remaining spots on the shelves contained the raw materials, fasteners, and hand tools that shops would need to maintain the factory and make the next generation of tools and die. It was the dad's job to check tools in and out and keep track of inventory for the craftsman who would need them during theirs.

The dad was the only person in the building who knew where each of these tools was located and could find them very quickly. The company learned the hard way that the Tool Cage inventory absolutely could not be lost or misplaced. Because of that, the entire cage was his private vault, protected by strict company rules, that only he and his immediate supervisor may enter. In theory, his boss also knew where things were. But the dad did this job so well for so long that, in practice, the boss had long since stopped paying attention to where things were.

Everyone in the factory thought that the dad had a mysterious, savant-like ability to remember where everything was. In truth, the system was the Dewey decimal system used in any public library, and his boss had installed it long ago. Each tool had an author, the craftsman who made it. That craftsman worked in a department, so each department had a range of numbers. Research and Development was 001–099, Fabrication was 100–199, and so on. Each tool had a made-on date and a title based on its first project in use. Since no one else was allowed in the cage, none of the guys in the factory had a chance to figure out his system. The workers in this factory did not use their library cards very often, so even fewer would recognize the system from its real source. After twenty years, the dad had memorized the contents of the cage and the location of everything in it.

Before he had the gate open that day, a small group had gathered to pepper him with questions and comments. Mercifully his boss appeared a short while later and chased them all away. But the boss just wanted the dad all for himself and immediately started asking all the same questions that the guys in the group did. But like his neighbor, the boss had watched the events at the park at least ten times and knew what happened much better than the dad did, so his excitement led him to answer all the questions himself. The boss did not know that the dad had not yet seen even a single replay and had only a vague idea of what had happened.

Not everyone in the factory was a baseball fan, so the rest of his day was normal. Twenty minutes of sitting in the cage in silence were typically interrupted by the five-minute process of checking a tool in or out. This process began with a few minutes of chitchat, followed by a formal request for a specific device. The dad would then roll his heavy table down the appropriate aisle to fetch the tool.

The table was hefty, and it had thick, black wheels that could be locked in place with a foot brake. One of its wheels had a chunk missing from it, so with each revolution, it would let out a loud *clunk* sound. They had tried to replace the table fifteen years ago, but since it was at least seventy-five-years-old, a modern replacement of as high quality was not findable. The clunking noise had become kind of a locator mechanism for those waiting at the gate that allowed them to monitor his progress as he moved about in the bowels of the cage.

The tabletop was about two feet by three feet, and the thick steel top was heavily pitted and scratched by decades of interaction with heavy steel parts banging into it. On one side of the table was a long lever that was about eighteen inches in length. When the dad reached the shelf with the tool he needed, he could pump that lever up and down to activate the hydraulics that would raise the tabletop to the shelf level the device was on. He would then lock the wheels and slide the tool onto the table. Twisting the handle counterclockwise would release the hydraulics, and the table would gently lower back down to the travel position. He could then roll the table back to the gate, where they would slide the tool onto another cart that the worker could then go to his work station. Most tools were made of solid steel components, and even if they were small, they were always quite heavy. This process repeated itself for the rest of the day.

But today was all about his exploits at the game. Even if a man came to the cage with a real tool request, each visitor wanted to ask the same questions and hear the same stories. For the first time in his life, the dad was the center of attention, and he was enjoying it.

THE CALL

His wife was gathering the mail as he pulled into the driveway. The mom was excited to tell him about walking into the bank with a big check and trying to deposit it. The teller at the bank was happy to hear the story of where it came from because the wife was proud of her big-headed husband's exploits. Playing along, the teller finally pointed out he had forgotten to sign the check, so she could not deposit it without an endorsement. Neither knew that the dad had given the administrator at the ballpark direct-deposit information, so all that was taken care of. The mom didn't realize the big check was just part of the show. Still, the mom enjoyed the attention she got carrying it in and out of the strip mall where her family's bank was located.

The mom and dad had not yet discussed what they would do with all that money, but the mom had spent the better part of the day thinking about all the things they could do with the cash. That deck in the backyard needed replacement, as did their old riding lawn mower, but the mom desperately wanted a new fridge and stove and hoped to convince the dad to use the money for that.

As he pulled into the drive, she gathered up the big check and went out to greet him in the driveway. She put the big check on the hood of the car and was waiting excitedly with a pen as she asked him to sign it, bubbling all the while about what they should buy. He proudly signed it just for the show of it as she carried on with her wish list. He smiled, letting her dream, before explaining he already deposited the money. He then teased her, offering a purposefully stupid wish list designed to make her squirm while he worked through his list of dumb ideas. Finally, he said, "Honey, all I want is a half-dozen new Wiffle balls and two brand-new bats. Let me get that, and you can spend the rest on whatever you want!"

With that, she jumped to hug him in a way she hadn't done in twenty years. While he held her and appreciated the warm moment, privately he thought, "Damn, this hurts!"

It was about 7 p.m., and dinner neared completion. The boy was meticulously gnawing on the last of his chicken nuggets when the phone rang. The dad, still annoyed by the strange phone calls he had received, was exhausted from the excitement and pain of the last twenty-four hours and did not want to talk with anybody. He gestured a request that the wife answer and whispered, "I'm not here."

She picked up the handset and said in a chipper voice, "Hello! . . . Yes, it is. . . . No, he's not here right now. Can I take a message?"

The dad leaned in while the boy continued to gnaw on his nuggets.

"Really?" said the mom as she listened on, excitement rising in her voice "Really? . . . Oh, how exciting. . . . Yes, he will. . . . I promise. . . . Yes, he will! . . . Yes. I can speak for him. . . . That sounds great. . . . Fantastic! . . . Wonderful! . . . Absolutely. . . . OK, thanks for calling, I will make sure that he calls you tomorrow. . . . First thing. . . . Yes. . . . Yes. . . . Goodbye now." She softly placed the phone back in its cradle, like she was setting down a bomb that was ready to blow up.

Feelings of doom swept over the dad as she exploded back toward him with all the excitement and power of a twenty-year-old cheerleader. "Honey, they want you to bat again! They want you to come back and hit another home run and then we can win another five thousand dollars and get a new porch and new mower. You can hit another one, right? You can, right? And maybe a Jacuzzi, and . . ."

THE MIRROR

As the crust loosened from his eyes enough for him to open them, the dad found himself overwhelmed with the feeling of dread. He laid there a few minutes imagining what the day might hold for him. Finally, he glanced over at the clock as the time clicked over to 9:10 a.m. Luckily this was a Saturday so he didn't have to work today and he went about his morning ritual entirely consumed with thoughts of how he could avoid trying to bat again. "It's two days later, and I still hurt—why would I want to do that again?" he thought. He cycled through various scenarios and considered all possibilities while he showered, shaved, and dressed. In the end, feigning injury seemed like the best approach. "No one could question that," he thought.

He stood there with a bent arm, holding his razor as he leaned into the mirror, suddenly frozen while he studied himself. Vanity was never a vice for him, but now he marveled at how ridiculous his big bald head was when compared to his scrawny body. "How is it possible that I have no muscles?" he thought.

Now standing straight, he shifted from side to side—he had never noticed that one nipple seemed slightly higher than the other, and he tried to remember if it had always been that way. There was also an odd patch of hair on his chest that was very gray in a way the rest was not. "What's that about?" he thought.

After a defeated exhale, he stood looking himself in the eye for the longest time, considering his options. A drop of blood appeared on his cheek and moved slowly down his face as he whispered to himself, "I can't do this—"

Breakfast was unusually quiet. The mom could feel how preoccupied he was. Finally, she blurted, "So are you gonna do this? It really can't hurt. What's the worst that can happen?"

He looked at her and said, "Honey, you know there is no chance at all that I'm gonna do it again—right?" He paused for what seemed like minutes. "It was an accident; you know that, right? I could get ten thousand more swings and never—"

They looked at each other as the boy clinked his spoon in search of the last of his cocoa puffs. There was a long stillness between them until eventually the dad said, "I just don't want to disappoint you."

With that, the boy stood up and moved quickly to the dad, stopping close in front of him. Again, the parents watched as the boy's gaze lifted a bit—not in full eye contact, but as close as either parent had ever seen. Tears appeared in the mom's eyes as the boy gave a tiny nod to his dad. As they watched the boy turn and go outside, the dad exhaled.

"OK, I'm gonna have to get some baseball shoes."

THE SHOE STORE

I t was not quite 11 a.m. and the mall was not yet crowded on this Saturday morning. The mom led the dad through the halls of the mall as though he were a condemned man being dragged to the scaffold. The dad hated the place, even though it was his wife's sacred space. The family walked past dozens of storefronts as the mom narrated all the way. They were in front of the sporting goods store and stood looking inside. After a long moment, he said, "OK, let's get some shoes," and started toward the store.

"Hey, why don't I go over to the appliance store while you guys do this? That OK, honey, do you mind?" she said with a big smile, and off she went, happily leaving him to the drudgery of buying baseball cleats that he didn't want and would only wear once.

Not only was the dad bowlegged, but his shoe size was incredibly tricky to find: size nine, triple D. He also had a bunion on his right foot that he had never bothered to treat. For all his adult life, the dad had always worn the soft, casual shoes made for people with diabetes. He suspected that they did not make diabetic baseball cleats.

After about ten minutes of looking at baseball cleats alone, a salesman approached and tried to greet him. The dad interrupted and asked: "Do you have any baseball shoe size nine, triple D?"

The salesman looked at the boy. "Are you sure you have the right size? Why don't we give a quick measure? Come on over here and sit down and let's make sure." When the dad sat down, a look of shock overwhelmed the salesman's face. "Oh, baseball shoes for you. Are you sure?"

"Ya, I guess so," said the dad, sheepishly."

With a knowing smile, the salesman slid a red vinyl and chrome tube stool used for fitting shoes in front of him and sat down. The dad slid off his right shoe and offered his foot for consideration. "Oh my God!" The salesman recoiled at the sight of the bulging bunion.

Then, reclaiming his last shred of professionalism, the salesman pretended shoes might exist to fit these feet and went through the dance of measuring the dad's foot's length and width, even though they both knew the futility of it. The salesman then disappeared in search of a shoe size no one had ever requested. As the dad waited, he watched the boy playing with the laces on an expensive pair of neon-orange, patent-leather baseball shoes.

After an eternity, the salesman returned, shaking his head, and explained that triple D was just an incredibly wide size. They only had one pair in the store, and they were size thirteen. He told the dad that they were special order shoes that were never picked up and had been sitting in the backroom for a couple of years. The dad paused to consider his options, then had an out-of-body experience as he heard himself say, "OK, let's try them on."

The salesman gave him a polite nod and a wry smile, then disappeared to fetch them. As the dad waited, a strange foreboding swept through him, a dread beyond the pale, like a teen in a tux at a shotgun wedding knows: trying it once changes your life forever. The salesman returned, sat down in front of him, and began the business of fitting the shoe. He slid open the box to the size thirteen triple Ds.

"Of course, why not?" the dad thought, as the neon-orange, patent-leather shoes spilled like lava from the box.

"Size thirteen?" he said. "That's all you thought to tell me about them? Did you notice they are orange?"

But this pair was different than the ones his son was

playing with. The spikes were molded rubber and not the steel cleats MLB players used. "That's good—I'm less likely to hurt myself," he mused to himself. They were also the only high-top baseball shoes he had ever seen. "Special order," he thought, pausing to consider why in the world anyone would ever special order such eyesores.

"So how long have you been playing baseball?" said the salesman, trying to make small talk as he laced up the molten monstrosities.

"Not very long," said the dad under his breath.

The dad was surprised that the shoes indeed felt fine when the salesman interrupted his thoughts. "OK, go on, walk in them see how they feel." He gave the left shoe a tap with the tip of his finger.

The boy came over quickly as the dad stood up and stared down at the shoes. The boy could see high energies on the surface of these shoes and studied them to make sure those energies were friendly. He watched as the rhythms rolled gently inward toward the father's foot, and he knew at once that they liked the father and could be trusted. He then drifted away so that they may better bond with the father.

The dad took a few steps and then stopped when he noticed several sales associates chuckling off in the distance. "These are great. I'll take them." And he sat down and quickly removed the hot lava from his feet while asking about the cost.

"Three hundred and forty dollars?"

The dad recoiled at that obscenity, so the salesman quickly adjusted the offer: "But we can give them to you for seventy dollars today only."

They completed the transaction, and the shoes were in the bag when the mom appeared next to the dad. "You found some?"

Tight-lipped, the dad nodded in the affirmative.

"That's great! Were they expensive?"

The dad and the salesman looked at each other.

"We gave him a great deal," said the salesman. "Have a

good day and come back soon."

The dad looked at him, and they each offered another knowing glance, like teenagers who had put out their cigarettes just in time before a parent entered the room. Walking out, the dad looked back to see a crowd of salesmen turning away to hide their laughter.

COSTCO

It was early Saturday afternoon and Costco was pretty packed at this time of day. The husband handed the server a five-dollar bill and recoiled a bit when the server gave him his food and put two dollars back in his other hand. Like a palm reader, he puzzled at the contents of his hand and shook his head in disbelief. "Thank you," he said, turning away with the food as he moved toward his family.

His two little girls waited in the bottom of the supersized grocery cart and squealed at the arrival of their hot dogs and pop.

"Look at that, two big hot dogs and two big drinks for three dollars?" he said to his wife, "How do they do that? At work, we would charge twenty dollars for that, and our hot dogs are half the size."

"Maybe that's why nobody is coming to your games," she said with a wry glance directed his way.

He stopped and stared at her dumbfounded. "I thought you liked bringing the kids to our games."

"I do, but we get to sit in a private suite and eat free food. If we had to pay twenty dollars for a hot dog, I would hate that too," the wife shot back privately, laughing at him a bit.

He was startled at her sudden willingness to offer these insights. "So, you only want to go to the games for free food and private box."

"No, I love baseball, and you—and I want to support you."

He looked at her disapprovingly. "Don't give me that look; I played college ball. I love the sport for itself, and I will always want to go to games."

"Then I don't understand. What's your point?"

"Well, I'm married to the assistant general manager of the Detroit Tigers, so that ballpark is our livelihood." She paused to allow him to consider what she was saying.

"Soooo—go on. Don't get shy on me now," he said, looking at her.

"Well, if I was Jane Q Public, and my husband didn't make a half-million dollars a year, there is no way I would want to pay twenty dollars for a hot dog. There is no way I would pay eight dollars for a bottle of water only to watch a terrible baseball team. Twelve dollars for a beer—really?" She looked at him like it was his fault.

"But that's what we need to charge," he said defensively.

"Nooo—that's just what you're in the habit of charging," she said, cutting him off. "We just bought two hot dogs and two drinks for three dollars. I could buy the same food and make it at home for a dollar, so why do you guys charge twenty?"

"We've always done it that way."

"Ya, but that's stupid!" she fired back.

"You go, girl, tell me why," he said, playing along.

"Because!" she said, stomping her foot loudly.

His wife was a tall, slim, athletic woman. As a collegian back in 2005, she played third base for the softball team at the University of Michigan, the year the team won the national championship. She caught the foul fly ball that ended the game. Upon graduating with a Master's degree in social work, she moved on to work as a school counselor in the Detroit Public School system.

She met her husband at something called Tigerfest, when a group of her students attended the event. Tigerfest is a typical community outreach program that most teams offer in some version. Tigerfest allows the public to wander around parts of the stadium that they typically do not get to see, and go into places like the dugout, the clubhouse, and up to the press box. A few of the players and coaches show up, and it's generally a well-received event for the community, the players, and the staff. On that day, her husband-to-be was a low-level staff member.

They decided early on not to have kids right away, so she was almost thirty-five before it happened. When the twins were born, they both agreed that she would stay home with the babies and live the life of a stay-at-home mom and corporate wife.

The mom part was natural in that the twins were the mythical perfect children and never gave their parents any problems. As babies and toddlers, they slept through the night, never got sick, played with each other, and didn't seem to be too demanding. Now, seven years old and about to start school, they were happy little girls who loved hanging out with their mom and eating hot dogs at Costco.

The corporate wife part of their relationship was much more difficult for her. It required her to straddle the supportive wife role by muting her own distinct personal experience and opinion—at least in public. The difficulty for her, first and foremost, was the male-dominated world of professional sports, populated with men whose views of women were still three centuries behind.

The first group of men she learned to tolerate were the former athletes or players who hung on with the team after their careers were over. They often served ambassadorial roles within which they were assigned a central focus, usually public relations or scouting.

Most of these ambassadors had been great players once. All of them started playing professionally in the minor leagues right out of high school, and playing, or training to play, baseball was all they had ever done. While there were exceptions, for the most part, they had no real-world skills or actual knowledge of how to do anything beyond baseball, but they did have an opinion on everything.

It was her experience that they were arrogant, spoiled, and self-centered. Sadly, their wives were even worse. She did not like that because in her world of women's college athletics the women studied, played, and worked hard. Most of all, they took care of each other. These guys and their wives did none of those things.

The second group of men that she found intolerable were the business people. These guys all had significant smarts, excellent educations, business experience, and managerial expertise. These were the people who ran the business side of what was an almost billion-dollar corporation, yet, they had little interaction with the coaches and athletes that were the products that they sell to the public. These business guys did not attempt to, or at least spent very little time evaluating the actual quality of the team when setting ticket or product prices they sold to the public. Instead, their mantra was: prices always go up, never down, even if the product is crap. Wins were irrelevant. Winning for them was measured only in profits. This group shared a common trait with the first group in that while they may have never played the game, they were equally arrogant and opinionated.

But no amount of arrogance could be compared to the coaches and athletes that made up a professional baseball team. Pro baseball players were among the best athletes in the world and were incredibly insulated from the realities of the real world. They were given everything and paid outrageous sums of money, while supported and surrounded by the best medical, training, and support staff that money could buy, waiting on them hand and foot. The media continually glorified them, and most were so young they have no concept of life outside of baseball. The world of professional baseball was rarefied air that glittered and sparkled while viewed from the stands or TV, but it smelled like post-game socks if you got too close.

The corporate wife part was much more difficult for her because she was not without opinion, and didn't like being a wallflower wife. She understood her lot in life and played the role with grace and charm at parties. In truth, it wasn't all that bad, but there were times when she just wanted to let loose. But her husband was a great guy, with a great job making great money, and doted on his wife and kids.

He started at the organization as an intern with a business degree in college, and stayed with the company as an employee. Over the years, he found ways to make himself valuable, following the old-fashioned path of working his way up the corporate ladder. Over time he had become a respected, well-liked person of power on the administrative side of the organization.

She realized the foot stomp was a bit much, so after a pause, she calmed and said: "OK, follow this—five years ago, the team was in the playoffs, right?"

He nodded.

"The team was winning?" she continued.

He nodded again.

"People will pay those prices to see a winning team?"

"Of course," he said.

"Think about it, though—even then, you had empty seats, right?"

He nodded less happily, as he began to see the point.

"If people don't want to spend four hundred dollars when the team is winning, why would they do it when the team is crap?"

Defeated, he looked away.

"And they especially don't want to pay twelve dollars for a beer—ever." She knew that the last comment was the punch after the bell and regretted it immediately.

With a heavy sigh, he sunk into one of the great big recliners for sale at the front of the store. "

Why do you think we came to Costco today?"

He looked up at her. "I don't know—we need stuff?"

"Yes, we do, but we could get everything we need at the grocery store, and it's three miles closer."

She stopped and looked at their two kids happily munching on their hot dogs in the grocery cart.

He turned and watched them eat too.

"A dollar fifty. It gets us in the door," she said.

His head was spinning as she spoke.

"Think about this, OK? When I was a kid, my brothers

were Boy Scouts."

"OK? So? What's that got to do with this?" he said defiantly.

"Because every year, and sometimes twice, the Scouts would go to Tiger Stadium."

"We still have a Scout Day," he offered defensively.

"Yes, but you guys turn it into a great big corporate opportunity to sell stuff." She paused to consider how far to take this.

"Don't stop now. Tell me what you really think," he said, not actually wanting her to.

"When I was a kid, the Boy Scouts would go to Tiger Stadium with their bag lunch and not be forced to spend a dime beyond whatever it cost to get in.

They brought thermoses of lemonade, for God's sake. You don't even have drinking fountains."

He thought about what she was saying, then demonstrated that he clearly missed the point of it.

"Well, we can't allow that—we're a business, we have to make money."

Angered, she went on, "Ya but how much? And that's bullshit! The Tigers make money just from the TV contract before they ever sell a single ticket, and even if that weren't true, do you have Boy Scouts at the stadium these days? Or their older brothers? Or with their dates when they grow up? Or with their kids when they become parents? Any of those Boy Scouts making a return trip on their own anymore? Do you make money from empty seats, honey? Because you got a lot of them these days, and they look crappy on TV."

She paused and did a slow show circle before looking back at him. She sat in the recliner next to his.

"Costco gets butts in the door because the dollar-fifty hot dogs are regret free—I mean who cares about a dollar fifty—but once we're here we spend four hundred dollars on huge jars of mayonnaise we don't need, or on olive oil."

Both chuckled, and then there was a pause before she continued. "We went with the Scouts as kids, and that place was great fun, forty-nine thousand Boy Scouts beating on the seats and chanting for the Tigers to start a rally—and the Tigers were not good back then either. We might have gone the first time because of the Boy Scouts, but we went back because it was fun. We were fans of the experience. It was a pastime, win or lose—it was a pastime. Baseball isn't a pastime anymore; it's a corporate event, it's not fun if you're an average family making forty thousand dollars a year that has to pay four hundred dollars just to see a game and then another twenty dollars for a hot dog. That's a lot of regret for most families!"

After a pause, he looked down. He mumbled apologetically, "It's not four hundred dollars everywhere!" Then he slumped like a fighter who knew he was beaten.

She realized she just blew way past his ability to listen anymore and that this was a cruel beating. Their gazes drifted aimlessly around the room as she stood back up to allow him to regain his balance.

Mercifully, one of the girls stepped in, making noises at her and snapping her out of the stupor.

"Listen, honey, I'm gonna give you a minute, the girls and I are gonna go over to..." She waved in the general direction of the canned good area of the store. "Meet us in olive oil, OK?"

As she walked away with the girls, he turned his gaze to the hot dog line and pondered the twenty-five people waiting there.

THE SHOES

A vivid flashback woke him to the smell of red dirt filling his nose and the pounding sensation of a Mack truck sonic pulse as thousands laughed at him lying face down in a brightly lit field. He realized he was drenched in sweat and sat up in bed.

"You OK, honey?" said the mom in nighttime tones. The clock to his left let him know it was 2 a.m.

"Ya, just can't sleep," he whispered back. "I'm gonna get up and start over—OK?"

With that, he slipped out of bed and wandered out into the dark house, wondering what to do. Guided by an unseen hand, he eventually ended up outside and found himself standing behind his car, still in his mismatched pajamas.

As if in a trance, he popped open the trunk and reached for the bag of shoes. He opened the bag and slid open the box and instantly realized that these shoes glowed in the dark. "Why would anybody make glow-in-the-dark baseball shoes?" he thought.

He sat on the ledge of the open trunk and went through the motions of putting them on. The fourteen eyehole sets took forever to lace up, as if a cosmic confirmation that any individual going through that effort must genuinely want to put them on. He looked down at the things swallowing his feet and bent over to get a better look. "I'm gonna look like a clown!"

He stood up and looked around. He then took a few awkward, exploratory steps, paused, then did it again, like a young colt taking its very first steps. It all felt wrong, and the extra length of the shoe made it difficult for him to touch the ground right. He slowly shuffled around for a few minutes, trying to think of a way he could get out of this without disappointing his family.

Emboldened by a sudden exuberance that all young colts must feel, he started to jog. When he reached one edge of the yard, he stopped, turned back toward the car, and did it again, each time trying to move a bit faster.

He did this for a few minutes and was starting to gain some confidence when he heard a loud baritone voice. "What the heck do you have on your feet?" said their neighbor. "And what in God's name are you doing?"

The dad was so startled he peed his pajama pants. "Nothing, just looking at the stars..." he said, quickly retreating to the safety of the darkened garage.

Once safely inside, he pressed the automatic door opener button on the wall. The garage light came on, fully illuminating him. He turned to see the neighbor staring at the shoes and his wet pants in stunned silence as the door mercifully closed to separate them. When door stopped, the neighbor thundered on with a series of excited questions.

"Hey, what are those shoes for? Did you wet your pants, buddy?" As if they were still in the same room.

The neighbor continued to look at him through the garage door window and didn't slow for breath while the panicked dad spastically clawed at the shoes to get them off. He hid them behind a bag on top of the beer fridge before disappearing back in the house just as the automatic light switched off.

FAMILIAR FACES

The game would be a few days later and when they arrived at the ballpark than night, the dad sensed something different. He assumed that this night at the ballpark would be much like all the other times there, just watching a game with his kid with a brief interruption during the seventh inning stretch. He usually could find free parking quickly near the park, but tonight it took much longer and all the ordinarily no-cost parking lots were charging a five-dollar fee.

The dad had made a point of not telling anyone at work about tonight in a naive attempt to keep them from finding out about it. He thought he had pulled it off, but as they approached the curved awnings of the entrance, he could see a large crowd of familiar faces. The mom usually did not go to games with her boys, and in truth, she wasn't there for the game this time either. She had organized an enormous surprise outing at the ballpark with family, friends, and a lot of the dad's coworkers. The only one who did not know about it was him.

Upon seeing him, the large crowd opened up like the Red Sea, forming a path for him to walk through. The crowd of friends clapped and cheered, slapping his back as he walked by, but he felt like a boxer being led to sacrifice against a heavyweight champ. He kept his head down, a scared, novice flyweight paraded to his fate, all the while forcing a big ole bug-eyed smile.

The dad looked up and realized that at the end of his row Blazer Dude was standing in a spotlight, holding a microphone and looking at the dad with mischievous intent. Men with TV cameras surrounded him and everyone stood to allow Blazer Dude pass or to bear witness to the spectacle that was about to happen. Once he reached the dad, Blazer Dude shifted into Las Vegas Master of Ceremonies mode, loudly launching into a long, embarrassing speech about lots of tickets sold, people wanting him, batting, fabulous this, special that, how great he would do, and all things gorgeous and fantastic, on and on. Blazer Dude proudly announced they would come to get him and all his friends at the end of the fifth inning and take them all to a special batting practice session under the stands before he had to hit. The dad was utterly embarrassed by the attention.

The last time he batted, he had the benefit of having no idea it was about to happen, with no time to think about it, practice, or warm up. In contrast, he had thought of nothing else for the last week. He had counted on a few minutes of quiet beneath the stands to put on his cleats and stretch a bit before going out to bat. He planned to keep his head down, strike out in three pitches to keep the wife happy, and go home. Now, that plan had turned into a circus. The first five innings were a blur. He sat oblivious to everything else, dreading the embarrassment. He was mortified of being forced to warm up and practice in front of a bunch of coworkers who had never seen him swat at a fly, let alone a ball. When the fifth inning ended, he was dripping with sweat, even though he had not moved in almost ninety minutes.

Suddenly his wife stood up and beamed at him like a lovesick teen. Immediately all of his buddies got up en masse and started moving toward the aisle. Blazer Dude appeared behind him, bent down in his ear, and said, "Let's go, champ." He rose up slowly like a condemned man trying his hardest not to cry, hugging his box of shoes as he walked to the gallows.

He was the last person in the parade to arrive at the chamber beneath the stands. The area was a relatively sizeable concrete space lined with scattered palettes of boxes and a few golf carts. The ceiling was a series of large slanted concrete beams that matched the slope of the seats above.

The team had set up a batting practice area lined with crowd-control ropes festooned with bunting, flags, and helium balloons tied every few feet. There was also a batting cage, pitching mound, and one of the team's pitchers and a catcher waiting for his attention. Worst of all were the bright lights from the two local news crews sent to cover the event.

His friends clung eagerly to the back of the batting cage, looking at him with stupid smiles and nonstop chatter and advice. He stood there ready to cry, when suddenly the solution hit him. "I have to use the men's room—give me a minute."

With that, he quickly disappeared into a tiny unisex bathroom just inside the hallway that led to the field. He locked the door and slumped to the ground, backed up against the door, trying not to throw up. After a few minutes, he heard his wife's voice at the door. "Honey, is everything OK?"

The boy watched the bathroom door from across the hall. He knew his father was feeling ill and was happy that the shoes were there to comfort him.

Still hugging his box of shoes, the dad looked back at the door and replied, "Yep—give me a minute." Then he saw the light switch, so he reached up and pulled it down, plunging the room into darkness. He sat there, eyes shut, listening to his heart race and dreading the next twenty minutes he now realized there was just no way to avoid. His head sagged into his chest, and as he opened his eyes, he realized that there they were, glowing, the perfect shoes to put on in a dark room—even the laces glowed in the dark! He sat for the next fifteen minutes, lit only by that glow, listening to his friends at the door whispering theories about what might be going on inside the bathroom. Finally, he put on his neon, high-top, glow-in-the-dark, patent-leather baseball cleats. Then, in the distance, he could hear the blazer dude say: "Where is he—is he ready?"

Beyond that, he heard the loudspeaker announce the last out of the inning. He turned on the light, got to his feet, and stood there, looking at his big orange feet, waiting for the knock he knew was coming. It came, and he heard the loud, clear voice of the blazer dude say, "Let's go, champ."

He opened the door, and immediately those huge shoes exited the bathroom, proudly taking him right past Blazer Dude and on to where he needed to go. First, the cleats did a crisp left turn, so he followed them with his head down, admiring their beauty, always focused on those majestic orange shoes as they marched him up the hall. They moved him onto a ramp, through a gate, and then proudly paraded themselves onto the field, stopping in the batter's box just as the speaker was announcing his name.

The boy watched as the dad came out of the tunnel and approached him. He was happy to see the dad was glowing soft and warm, even if he did have a few jerky, nervous echoes following him. The fragments in the shoes were very excited and proud, and the boy could see clearly how the cleats protected him and how the darker shadows blurred as they approached.

The protective screen was in place and that his boy was safely behind it with the mom, so the dad stood there confidently, waiting for someone to hand him a bat. The team's batboy appeared with a helmet and a bat, and this time the batting helmet fit perfectly, and the bat was brand new. He stood there, sweat dripping off his big bald head, bulging eyes, bowed legs, dressed in green shorts, blue shirt, and the great big shiny glow of the dark-orange shoes. He looked over at his boy and heard the same umpire as before yell, "Play ball!"

Back in the yard earlier in the day, his boy was throwing wicked curveballs, each break bigger than the last, and he did not hit a single one of them, not one in forty-five minutes, as his boy easily won all three games. He marveled at the boy's improvement, at how much fun he had playing with him, and how good the boy had become. It made the dad proud.

Earlier that day, the boy threw to his father as carefully as he possibly could, as if pitching to a toddler, but was sad because his father could not hit the ball. The father was a very slow learner, and he could not seem to grasp how easy hitting a thrown ball was. The boy repeatedly told his father that the secret to hitting a thrown ball was to not watch the ball! The dad could not seem to understand that the key was watching the negative space around the ball and its plasma pushing patterns out of the way as it moved through the air. Patterns make trails as they jump out of the way; the ball will end up at the end of the trail, so wait at the end and the hitting is easy. "If only he could listen better."

The father took his stance and gave a wink at his boy, then instantly backed out of the batter's box when he noticed what the boy was doing. He has seen the boy do this a million times but was shocked to see him do it at this moment. His boy was flapping his hand that very distinct way that he did when the next pitch would be a breaking ball. He was clearly waving his fingers downward like someone testing the temperature of bathtub water. "Could it be?"

He stepped back in the box and looked out at the pitcher with his big ole bug eyes, and the pitcher went immediately into his windup. The dad's heart settled, and he was suddenly calm, calmer than he had been in two weeks. He saw the Rawlings label on the ball as it spun out of the pitcher's hand. Wide eyed, he studied the rotation as the logo formed a tightly spinning little dot. He swung, then dropped the bat and raised both his hands high over his head. He stood there breathless and still, watching the flight of the ball as it arched majestically away from the plate. He watched as the center fielder turned and then stopped to watch the baseball as it disappeared over the Miller Lite sign on the wall in center field.

He stood in the pose two or three seconds longer, looking out at center field. Suddenly, he was snapped back to reality by the explosive sounds of the pitcher approaching him. "Who the hell do you think you are, showing me up that way, you run dammit, before I pound the crap out of you!"

The pitcher was in absolute rage and was approaching fast and hard, fixing to kick the dad's butt. Instinctively the dad retreated, and just as the pitcher raised his fist to deliver a monster punch, the catcher moved between them. The two young men wrestled to the ground. Immediately the first and third basemen piled on to control the furious man. Some other players grabbed the dad from behind and quickly led him off the field and back down the ramp, away from the chaos.

A swirl of bodies filled the area, and in that confusion, his glasses got knocked off. He stumbled into a wall and backed against it, aware of all the bodies and noise before him but unable to discern a single face. The cacophony of voices grew, and he was in a near panic when he felt someone grab his hand and realized it was his boy. Suddenly the world came into view as his wife's face appeared smiling in front of him. She slid the spare glasses on his face, the ones she always carried for him.

"Nice shoes!" she said as an ocean of people moved around them. They looked at each other a long time before looking down and smiling at the boy.

"Can we please go home now?" the dad whispered.

ICE CUBES

The dad's journey through the kitchen toward was interrupted by the muffled sounds of giggles and happy voices coming from the backyard. His wife was not in her usual spot when he came home from work, and these sounds were new to him, so he stood still as a spy might do to learn which guests his wife had invited over. He reached for the fridge to grab a beer and realized that standing before him was a brand-new stainless-steel refrigerator.

Their old fridge really was quite awful. It was at least twenty-five years old and had more things wrong with it than right. Both handles on the front ripped off long ago. It took forever to make ice, and they had to use those little plastic trays. But since there were no longer shelves in the freezer, that wasn't always possible. Inside, the fridge was dingy, and some of the plastic walls were cracked. Worst of all was that it didn't really shut correctly unless you pressed it really hard. If you did not, the cold air would spill out. Most of all, the old fridge looked like him, tired and beat up.

He pressed the ice-dispenser lever with a finger and out dropped a bunch of perfectly formed ice cubes. "Wow," he whispered. He opened the door to looked inside and was blinded by a high-intensity gleam that came from the shine of the surface. He shut the fridge and realized a new stove has also moved in right next to it.

"Looks like the appliance fairy has been busy today," he thought with a smile and he had to admit that it was pretty exciting to have new appliances. He moved toward the sound of voices, slid open the patio door, and looked towards the sounds. On this gorgeous Michigan afternoon he first saw the boy sitting out in the yard on the new riding mower. To his right his wife spoke: "Hi, honey, the water's fine. Come on in, join us," as she and her two friends giggled in the waters of a bubbling, beautiful, brand-new Jacuzzi. "Honey, this is pretty great. Do you think they'll let you bat again?" she said, laughing as her friends tittered on.

'No, I'm quite sure my baseball days are over" said the dad as he sat down to enjoy the company of family and friends. It had been two weeks since the dad's second at bat at Fifth Third Field. The pitcher that day got suspended for three games for fighting when he punched a player who was trying to calm him down. His suspension would one day make him the topic of a rather elaborate trivia question:

"Who is the only player ever to get kicked out of a game for hitting a teammate, while pitching for a team he wasn't on, pitching to a player not on any team roster?"

It turns out that the pitcher was only there that day on a rehab assignment and wasn't officially on the Mud Hens roster at the time. While this pitcher's memory would now be forever fused to one absurd moment of baseball trivia it does not come close to being the most outlandish of baseballs improbable events. Of all the great sports, baseball is king of keeping track of its measurables and trivia and each is carefully measured, recorded and celebrated.

There are many stories that litter baseball trivia and history about teams doing things to get fans into the park. The absolute worst was dreamed up by The Altoona Curve, the Double-A affiliate of the Pittsburgh Pirates, when it hosted "Awful Night." The goal of the event was to give the fans a bad experience at the ballpark. To that end, the first thousand fans were given a photo of the general manager's gallbladder. The grand prize, given to just one fan, was the general manager's actual gallbladder.

The absolute master of baseball trivia and promotional

events was a man named Bill Veeck. Back in 1951 Mr. Veeck was the owner of the Saint Louis Browns. He was known for many things, including thinking of himself as a showman in the style of P.T. Barnum. He had a long career as a baseball owner, and during that time, he came up with a lot of crazy promotional events. Two of the most memorable included the decision to have announcer Harry Caray sing "Take Me Out to the Ball Game" during the seventh-inning stretch of Chicago Cubs games.

But Veeck's craziest brainstorm happened in August of 1951. Eddie Gaedel weighed sixty-give pounds and stood just 3'7" inches tall, so Bill Veeck decided to have him come out of a papier-mâché cake to become the shortest person ever to bat in a Major League Baseball game. Gaedal's plate appearance came during the second game of a doubleheader, and he walked on four pitches. He was immediately replaced with a pinch runner, and received a standing ovation from the eighteen thousand plus people in the stands that day. This was his only Major League plate appearance, and Mr. Gaedel never played again.

As the dad sat on the patio, visiting with his wife and friends, listening to the wonderful sounds of giggles and Jacuzzi bubbles he had no idea that at that moment, an administrator back at Fifth Third Field was about to get a phone call.

THE BOARDROOM

It had been a couple of weeks since the mother of twins taught her husband, an assistant GM with the Detroit Tigers a thing or two about what normal people want when the go to see a baseball game. He was stunned by the clarity of her thought and since that lesson he had been torturing himself mentally in an effort to think ways to make a bad baseball game more fun for people buying a ticket. He now had a few ideas but they were very unusual and he feared the ramifications if the Tigers brain trust gathered with him in the room today did not like them.

The Detroit Tigers were terrible that year and on pace to lose over ninety games. Attendance was at an all-time low, and generally there was not much community interest in the team. The local newspaper no longer put Tigers scores on the front page of the sports section, and that was something they had done for a hundred years. At this point, the reasons didn't matter. The Tigers needed to do something to get butts in the seats.

This meeting was about that side of the business, increasing sales revenue. The boardroom was clean and modern, with large glass windows overlooking the colossal tiger sculptures and the front entrance to the stadium. The event was passing the two-hour mark. As of yet, nothing was accomplished, except that everyone was getting annoyed with each other. Brainstorming consisted of stale suggestions of the usual Bat Day, Ball Day, Hat Day nonsense. The collective opinion in the room was that until the team was better, "What could we do?"

Finally, the assistant GM and husband to the mother of

twins summoned his courage and announced, "I have a couple of stupid ideas. One that's so bad we probably—well, the league won't even let us try it." With that, the room fell silent, and everyone sat up in their seats.

"I like bad ideas!" said a peer.

"Ya, the worse, the better, as far as I'm concerned," said another.

"Fire away," said the big boss. "What can it hurt at this point?"

The assistant manager shuffled the papers in front of him and took a quick measure of the room. Everyone was looking at him, and he realized that this could really be awful.

"OK, I'll start with the worst idea first because they will never allow it anyway. Does anyone here know who Eddie Gaedel is?"

"That's it? Midgets? You wanna bring back midgets? I don't think we can get that by the PC police, do you? Come on!" said the prickly guy from across the table as everyone laughed.

"He's right. We're not doing midgets," said the big boss.

The assistant GM jumped back in, as if he suddenly had a great deal of confidence in his plan. "No, no, listen please! Hear the whole plan and then tell me I'm wrong."

And with that, the others indulged him. "I understand that the Eddie Gaedel thing was a stunt—disgusting, stupid, non-PC, but also a very incredible trick. It was beautiful because it made that stadium on that day fun. And that's what we need to do, make our stadium fun, even if the team is not winning. We need to make it a place where people want to come just because of the environment, independent of the success of the team.

"By the way—Eddie Gaedel really was a great stunt, and the fans in the stadium loved it that day. The White Sox got a huge bump in attendance the next two weeks just because of that one at bat. But let me start over, let me be clear. No, I don't want to bring in midgets, that was a bad reference. I want to bring back the fun. I want to bring in the modern equivalent, I want to bring in Quasimodo!" As he said that, he stopped and looked at the faces around the room, and every one had a sour look on it.

"Quasimodo? The cartoon hunchback? Dammit, we can't bring in hunchbacks, cartoon or otherwise. We're also not gonna bring in trolls, giants, dragons or unicorns," barked the big boss.

"This is beyond terrible," said the prickly guy.

"No, no, that is not what I mean either. Listen, listen! Let me try again. That was a bad example too.

Do you guys remember a couple of weeks ago that stunt the Mud Hens pulled when they had that fat, bald, weird-looking guy with the orange shoes bat?"

"Ya, the dude hit a home run!" said another guy.

"Good! So, Sports Center gave him the nickname Quasimodo, that's all I meant, I'm talking about a real person OK? Well, did you know that when they brought him back for the second time, they advertised he was gonna bat again and with just three days' notice they sold five thousand extra tickets? Five thousand more tickets just on that one night. That stadium only holds ten thousand. It was incredible. And, after he hit that second home run, it was replayed all over the TV for the next two weeks. The only reason they didn't ask him back again was that they were afraid he would hit another home run, and they couldn't afford it."

Everyone in the room got quiet and settled down. Finally, someone said, "So, what are you suggesting, that we find a bow-legged fat guy and let him bat?"

"No. I'm suggesting we get that exact fat, bowlegged, bald guy, and we put him on the team."

The room went silent before the big boss decided to play along. "Well. OK. So let's say we do that, say it gets us five thousand more people for one night. What good does that do?"

"Well, I'm betting it won't be five thousand, based on all the national media he got. I bet if we advertise this right, we can get fifteen or twenty thousand! The guy is kind of a gargoyle, people loved him!" And again, there was a long pause in the room.

"OK, so we have a big night. What's that do for us we have fifty home games left?"

"So that's the beauty; it won't be just for one night!"

"How so? You think he's gonna hit the ball? That guy can't even run. I watched the replays, hotshot, Quasimodo's first at bat was a train wreck. I thought he was gonna die."

"Ya, and people watched it because it truly was a train wreck—but millions of people have seen replays of it, and it's only been two weeks since that second at-bat. That's a lot of free advertising already taken care of. We will announce that he's on the team and that we are gonna let him bat. By doing that, we are gonna instantly get fifteen or twenty thousand people wanting to witness that train wreck for themselves."

"OK, so, if we let him bat, and when he bats and strikes out and then it's all over, and that's it, no more twenty thousand people. You were right, this really is an awful idea."

The assistant GM paused to gather himself for the final push. "Ahhh, but that's just it. We put him on the team and announce some fancy slogan: 'Come watch the Bowlegged Wonder.' Doesn't matter what the slogan is, people will show up to watch the gargoyle get in a train wreck."

"Again, that's one night. How does that help us?"

"It's not one night, because we aren't gonna bat him the first night." Everyone sat back in their chair and began to see the plan.

"And then we don't bat him the second night, or third, or fourth night, but we go as long as we can and continue to advertise the hell out of it. We make up some stories that he got sick, or he can't hit lefties. I don't know, anything to give him a reason why he didn't bat. Then when the crowds die back down, we confirm that tomorrow night, he definitely, absolutely will bat, and we get the crowds back, and then I guess we pretty much have to let him bat. It doesn't matter because the point all along was to get butts in the seats and show them that our ballpark is a fun place to be. But we have to make it fun."

The room was silent for a long time as everyone sheepishly looked around, imagining the thousands of problems with the plan.

"The manager will never go for it."

"So what? We all know he wants out of here anyway."

Finally, one of the quieter members of the group offered: "Ya know, we have orange in our team colors, we could make the players wear orange shoes!"

The room grew in confidence as the members start to imagine the possibilities.

"Or we could pass out fake big bug-eyed glasses: 'Bug Eye Day.'"

"Or fake bald heads."

"Or have bow-legged races."

"Settle down," boomed the big boss as they started to get out of control. "There is no way the league is gonna allow this. Have you thought of that?"

"They have to. How can they not?" said the assistant GM.

"Just look at the guy! That's how," shot back the prickly guy.

"Yes, but look at what he did! We show them the two very long home runs he hit in the minor leagues, which he did, and they weren't cheap. He crushed them, and the second one was off a former all-star. Heck that guy played in the league for eleven years, he was the real deal. We tell them he is just going to be a pinch hitter."

"How do we justify financially putting this guy on the roster for a week if we're not gonna play him? The minimum is still a lot of money!"

"We've got seven guys on the roster right now that haven't played in ten days, and all of them are getting paid. Heck, most of them make a lot more than the minimum. This guy will be cheaper, and I bet he will agree to do it. He only makes thirty-two thousand a year at the factory he works at."

"Wait, if this is such a good idea, why didn't one of the other teams already get him? He's not under contract, anybody could have signed him."

"Because he is under contract—with us! When the Mud Hens do this stunt, they keep a roster spot open and actually sign these people to a contract for insurance reasons. After that person strikes out, they always release them right away. After he hit that second home run—well, they still haven't released him, so all we gotta do is buy his contract for nothing and call him up."

This couldn't be true! Everyone went quiet again and looked down at their notes or tapped their hands on the table.

"I have a question!" said the quiet guy.

"Ask!" boomed the big boss.

"You said you had a couple of stupid ideas? What are the others?"

THE OFFER

"So those are the details, and that is our offer. Do you understand what we are trying to do and what we need from you?" The dad gave a puzzled nod in the affirmative, and then there was a long pause as the mom and dad looked at each other.

Looking at their concerned faces, the assistant GM realized he had forgotten to cover the business topics. "Major League minimum pay is about twenty-three hundred dollars a day, and what we can pay you. You'll get paid for every day that you are on the team. Paydays are on the first and fifteenth of the month. We reserve the right to cut and release you at any time, for any reason, and there are no guarantees."

"While you're here, we'll give you an apartment to use, a per diem when you're traveling, as well as access to the team buffet, medical staff, and trainers. We plan to let you get used to things for six games before you bat, so if that works out, you will make about fifteen thousand dollars during that time, minus taxes. And, there is probably also some publicity and some interviews you'll have to do. Still, I'm betting it will be nothing serious. After that, we will release you, and you can go back to your life. So, what do you think? Wanna give it a try? You will be on the clock as soon as you sign the contract."

Spurred on by his wife's giggling, the dad leaned over the glass table, looked up at the man who was offering him a plate of gold, then signed the contract. Immediately his wife gave a string of tiny claps while jumping up and down in her seat, trying to not act too excited. The dad stood up, looked around the room, and asked, "What's next. What do I do—next?"

"Well, today's an off day, so how about I introduce you to my wife, and then we get you set up in the apartment and show you around. You're going to need to meet a few people."

THE APARTMENT

T he mother of twins was waiting for them in the hall. After introductions, they crossed the street outside the stadium to where the apartment was located. It was hidden on the second floor of a building that contained a five-story public parking lot and a sizeable live theater complex. Elevator access to the apartment was shared with people who might be returning to the parking lot or going to the theater. They waited for others as they got off on their floors, then the assistant GM inserted a key to take control of the elevator, and it began to move.

"Our players are typically a lot younger than you and tend to destroy things, so we usually put them in one of our offsite locations. But we thought, given your age, and how unique this situation is, we didn't think that would be a problem. We normally use this place for VIPs and parties, but it should work for you too. You're only going to be here for about a week, though, so don't get too attached to it." The elevator stopped, then the rear door slid open, revealing an elaborate art deco room.

"Follow me," said the mother of twins, leading the family out of the elevator. As it shut behind them, they stopped in front of a giant 1950s jukebox that was framed by large marble vases and even bigger gilded mirrors.

"Oh, this is really beautiful. This will be amazing. Are there beds through one of those doors?" said the mother of the boy.

"No, no, honey, this is just part of a hallway. That door

leads to the theater, and that one is to the parking garage," said the mother of twins, laughing a bit along with everybody else.

She then pressed the button of a small fob in her hand, and the jukebox rotated around and swung open like a fancy door in a science-fiction movie. Inside was a vast open space that was at least twenty-five feet tall and fifty or sixty feet long.

"Come on in. Let me show you around," said the wife as they walked inside.

"What is this place? Is this the hotel lobby? Is the apartment on this floor?" asked the boy's mother.

"No, the apartment is this floor. All this, this is the apartment," she said, smiling and giggling at the flabbergasted woman.

The apartment glowed with warmth, elegance, and sophistication. Immediately in front of them was a long leather couch with a sizeable tube-like backrest that separated the two sides. At either end of that were round, silver-lined, mirror-top tables surrounded by three crisp, red leather chairs with glossy black wooden arms. The wife led them into the room and pointed out some of the finer details. The entire length of the wall on the right was lined with beige calf's leather couches. Built into the armrest between each of these couches were thin golden chrome lamps that ended in elegant stained-glass sconces that bathed the wall in a soft glow. She pointed out the massive wall that was a mosaic of beautiful slate deco patterns. Above it all hung several large sunburst chandeliers.

The ladies and the boy drifted away from the men to explore the rest of the apartment. They walked toward the opposite wall and followed a colonnade of glowing golden glass tubes. These columns collectively formed a hallway that led to the living room, media room, game room, kitchen, and bar. At the end of the colonnade was a large spiral staircase that led up to the bedrooms. "Will you be joining your husband here for the week as well?

"Yes, I will!" bubbled the mom. "And our boy will too."

"You're gonna love it," said the perfect corporate wife.

The men watched as the ladies disappeared into other rooms.

"I need to go organize the rest of your day," said the assistant GM, "so I'm going to go do that, and I'll be back to get you in an hour. Take some time, look around. There is food in the fridge, kitchen's in there. Make yourself at home.

Is there anything else you might need?"

"Well . . ." said the dad. "Is there a place we can play Wiffle ball?"

THE HEAD COACH

The Kander and Ebb musical *Chicago* is full of outrageous characters and explores some of mankind's darker subjects, including murder, greed, and adultery. The story is told in a series of spectacular scenes that feature fantastic song and dance sequences performed by beautiful women and handsome men. In the middle of all that is a sad little character named Amos Hart. This pathetic character is the ultimate wallflower, and halfway through the second act, he sings a song called "Mr. Cellophane." In it, he details his pathetic, anonymous existence and the lengths he has taken to get noticed. He sings that his actions would have gotten anybody else in the world attention but him:

"Cause you can look right through me,

Walk right by me and never know I'm there."

Everybody has their people, their crowd, the ones that they are comfortable with. A person's comfort zone is usually populated with folks from the same social class, be it upper, middle, lower, whatever. Then people are also separated by education and areas of interest, hobbies, or the industry they work in, like theater, business, or athletics. While there is some movement up, down, or sideways within these groups, it usually happens slowly. If it happens quickly, it is nearly always through marriage.

Everyone knows an individual who is comfortable meeting new people or making new friends out of complete strangers. The dad, however, was not capable of either of these things, as he had always been very uncomfortable when put in a new environment.

One of the reasons he worked at the tool and die factory for twenty years was in part because it was comfortable for him. The people who worked for that company were all like him and had all been there for many years. There were seldom new faces to meet or remember, and he enjoyed that it was stable and very comfortable. It was his world, his people.

The only reason he agreed to do this baseball thing was the money, and even then, without the pushing of his wife, he would not have done it. The offer of half a year's salary for one week's work was too much to walk away from, so he figured he could put up with quite a lot for that much money. The one thing he did not think through, though, was all the new people he would be expected to meet.

A Major League Baseball team consists of several coaches and a roster of about twenty-five players. Beyond that, there are training and facility staff, doctors, administrators, players' wives, and on and on. As a player, he would not be expected to remember the names and faces of everybody he met. Still, even the names of the players were an overload to his system.

The assistant GM introduced him to the coaches first, and this introduction was perhaps the most awkward he had ever felt in his life. The head coach mechanically performed an introduction for each of his coaches. Each dipped their furrowed brows at him when cued, and each looked down on him like he was a strange talking lizard. In truth, he felt like one, so all he said to them was, "Nice to be here," not meaning a word of it.

Everyone in the room knew the plan before this meeting. The assistant GM nevertheless took the time to go through it with everybody in the room. They all knew this was done to make a point, and to make sure that the script was going to be followed. During this speech, the head coach was the perfect politician and looked at him with a crooked smile. However, the assistants in the background were less successful. They looked at the floor like third graders being forced to wait outside the principal's office. The assistant GM ended the meeting with a summation statement: "And this isn't up for discussion. Seven days from now, he will bat, at some point during the Cleveland game. Coach, you get to decide when that is, but he gets one at bat. Does everybody understand?"

With that, the head coach looked at the dad, smiled like the Cheshire Cat, and said, "I can't wait, really looking forward to it. Glad to have you on the team!"

After meeting the coaches, the assistant GM brought him out into the clubhouse to meet the players. If the coach's meeting was the most awkward experience of his life, then meeting the players was, well . . .it was ten times worse. Unlike the coaches, the players knew nothing about him or why he was there.

The assistant GM did not take the time for individual names, just a group announcement. "Hello, everybody! Listen up! Everybody! Please give me your attention." All the players in the room stopped and turned and looked in the general direction of the assistant GM. Eyebrows were raised in every corner of the room. On this team it was always the head coach who introduced new players.

"Everybody, this is our new pinch hitter. The plan is that he will be here for about a week, filling in for Johnson while he is on the DL. Please make him feel welcome." The GM gave him a big pat on the back and whispered, "OK, blend in. Get used to the place." And with that, he disappeared down the hall.

Standing before him were twenty-five men who were part of a unique fraternity of incredible athletes. All these men had spent years busting their butts, riding busses, and learning their trade in the minor leagues, fighting hard to earn their way to the spot in the room where he was now standing. Looking back at them was a strange, scared, middle-aged man in baggy white socks who did not have an athletic bone in his body. He felt like a calf in a room full of lions.

He gave the awkward wave of a fifth-grade boy at his first dance and put his hands in the pockets of his khaki shorts. He stood there, not having the slightest idea what to do for several long minutes, longing for the anonymity and protection of his tool crib. Not a single player bothered to introduce themselves. For that matter, not a single one even bothered to dip a furrowed brow his way.

He was the personification of Mr. Cellophane, and he was now completely invisible. Instinctively he looked around the room, acting like he was thinking hard about something or waiting for someone. Like a jock being forced to watch a ballet concert, he backed up as slowly as possible until finally he felt himself bump into a wall. He turned into the wall like it was completely normal and acted like he was reading the material on the bulletin board he had accidentally discovered. The bulletin board was covered with game schedules, hotel and travel information, a pay calendar, union and workplace safety notices, a request for players to sign up for a Special Olympics baseball thing, and a sign-up sheet for chiropractic and massage sessions, complete with a broken pen hanging from a string. All this was gibberish, and while he could read, he had little idea what any of it meant.

More than anything, looking at the bulletin board gave him a reason to kill time and be in the room without having to look at or interact with the players. It also allowed him to not see them looking at him while they whispered about him. Looking at the board also let him know that he was standing next to two doors that he realized could provide him an escape.

Not knowing where either went, he exited down the one on the right, traveled the length of a short hall, turned right again, and realized that he was in a large bathroom. When he entered the room, three players were doing what people do in a restroom. He had no actual need to be in the bathroom. But, he didn't want to be seen coming in and then immediately turning around, so he made his way to the very last stall, opened the door, and sat down to hide.

Major League Baseball players are used to players coming and going. But every player in the locker room knew in an instant that the dad was no baseball player. So, they started trying to figure out what was going on. On this team, the assistant GM seldom came into the clubhouse. If he did, he conducted his business in private, usually with the head coach. When the assistant GM called for everyone's attention to personally introduce someone nobody had ever heard of, alarm bells went off in every player's head. Clearly, this was no ordinary player, so in their effort to understand what they were seeing, they started making up scenarios to explain it.

One of the most popular theories among the players was that this dude had a lot of money and bought his way onto the team. While it is an outrageous theory, throughout history, wealth has allowed people to buy a way into and out of all sorts of situations. During a part of the civil war rich men were allowed to purchase a commutation that made it possible for them to avoid fighting in the war. A year after the Civil War ended a woman named Florence Foster Jenkins was born and she had the foresight to be born into a wealthy family. She was born in 1866, and it became a lifelong dream of hers to be a famous opera singer.

However, Florence Foster Jenkins did not sing well at all! Imagine the absolute worst singing voice you can possibly devise. Now triple all the qualities that make it terrible for you and that might begin to describe how bad the singing voice of Florence Foster Jenkins was. But when her father died, inheritance money meant that she was suddenly very well financed. So, Florence decided to become an opera singer, despite having no rhythm or musical ability.

She was known as the "Diva of Din" and lived her dream singing publicly from 1912–1944. Her audiences were a collection of loyal friends and curious musical types who just wanted to see if the legend about her stunningly bad singing voice was real. Apparently, though, she was a charming person and was clearly loved by her friends, who didn't have the heart to tell her how bad she was. She dismissed critics as being jealous of her. She went about happily living the life of an opera star for no other reason than because she loved to sing and had the money to pay for it. While none of these baseball players knew about the Diva of Din more than a few players believed that this odd-looking man must have a lot of money and had bought his way onto the team.

Professional baseball players are typically very jaded and in spite of being well compensated, live in a culture where they are bought and traded like commodities. They are moved around the country without regard to their personal wishes, often with little or no notice. They are used to seeing a new player arrive one day and be gone the next, so they tend to not get too invested just because someone new shows up in the room. But this guy was different. He didn't look like a ballplayer or even an athlete.

All athletes, baseball players included, can take one look at a person and tell right away if that person is a player. An athlete carries themselves differently than ordinary people do. Athletes don't even need to be doing anything at all to be instantly recognizable to each other, especially within the sub-categories of their sport. Wrestlers and gymnasts hold themselves differently than baseball or soccer players, but all athletes can recognize athletes at a glance. It was clear to all the players that this man, whoever he was, was no threat to their jobs, so they don't really care why he was there. He would be gone soon, and among those who talked about it, the consensus was to just ignore him.

GUERNICA

Paris of 1906 was filled with extraordinary artists. Rodin began his most famous sculpture, Klimt was starting to create abstract art, Manet was painting his *Water Lilies,* and Edvard Munch, Modigliani, Degas and Matisse were already acclaimed or in the process of creating seminal works that would define their careers. Yet, in an environment where extraordinary was normal, everyone knew that another artist stood apart.

People did not know what autism was at that time but recognized that this other artist was not normal. He seemed possessed by an internal presence that caused reactions to things others did not see. They could sense his inner haunting and knew he was both blessed and cursed with a visual acuity that inspired and tormented him with extraordinary images that teased at the edges of his reality.

This man had not yet created a single masterpiece, yet it was clear to all that, in time, he would create many. At twenty-six years of age, he had demonstrated rare artistic abilities, combined with a unique world view and a profound ability to allow his state of mind, both manic and depressive, to reflect in his work. He worked passionately to capture these visions, filling scores of pages with sketches in an insatiable quest to focus past the fog of life and on the vibrant world of his autistic perspective.

At the end of 1906, he bought materials to make a canvas for a painting that would change the world of art. Then, in the spring of 1907, he locked himself in his studio, and a few days later emerged with an extraordinary painting of five anonymous women depicted in a way that would make them unforgettable. Breaking every prior artistic convention, he rendered each woman as if seen from several perspectives simultaneously. Each face became primitive, almost masklike, with haunting black eyes that stared right back at the viewer, questioning their worthiness to judge, and challenging their bravery to maintain the gaze.

He waited several years to show Les Demoiselles d'Avignon to other artists because he knew how they would react. When he did, the painting was universally mocked, and he was personally vilified by his closest friends. Even so, its impact was immediate, and Cubism soon became a significant movement in the world of art.

Thirty years later, this same man had developed a full command of his autistic inner vision and used it to create perhaps the most potent antiwar painting of all time. It was his vision of the bombing of the town of Guernica during the Spanish Civil War. The huge colorless mural offered his view of people and animals suffering from the violence and chaos of war. The composition included a wounded horse, a bull, screaming women, body parts, and bombs bursting in air.

Lots of artists have painted the horrors of war, and most did it in a gruesome but realistic style. *Guernica* was totally different in that every element was swollen, distorted, or otherwise ripped apart in a way that was cartoonish, multi-perspectival, and horrible. Pablo Picasso had found a completely new, nonrealistic way to depict the horrors of war that was more terrifying and evocative than the most hyper realistic painting could ever aspire to.

History remembers both of these paintings as the work of a brilliant artist. It was his autistic mind that allowed the artist to see into another dimension populated by the beings we now see in his paintings. The man was haunted by the images in both of these paintings, and it was their grotesque quality that made him need to paint them. Picasso was painting the creatures and things he actually saw as he went about his life. Training and mechanical skills allowed Picasso to be a great painter, autism gave him the vision to be brilliant.

The boy also had autistic inspired visions, but before this point in his life, he was in control of them and had not yet experienced how powerful or disturbing they could be. Protected by his parents and the tall fence in his backyard, he had never been exposed to people who lived consumed by the Seven Deadly Sins. Now he was about to get his first glimpse of Envy, Pride, and Wrath.

TWO OLD MEN

A highly regarded construction supervisor who spent two years helping to build the stadium was the first person ejected from Comerica Park. He was actually in charge of building the entire stadium. In that position, he personally stepped in every square yard and knew intimately every detail about the place. Yet the field was viewed as so untouchable that, a few days before the stadium opened, Mr. James Wills stepped out onto the infield to have his photo taken and was instantly fired. They ejected and banned him for life from Comerica Park. Even today, the surface of the field is protected like Fort Knox, and nobody is allowed to step on it except players and the people who maintain it. However, this season, the GM himself made a unique point of allowing the dad and boy to use the field for their Wiffle ball games and told the staff to support it like any other team activity.

The boy stood out of the way against the wall in the right-field corner as the white shadows moved things into place. He liked the white shadows. When the faces of the white shadows got big at him, they smiled and talked in pretty tones and give him pleasant tastes. But right now, the boy was very concerned with the two dark shadows he could see watching him from the dugout on the other end of the field. Their eyes were very black, and they studied him hard, and the boy did not like them.

The dad and the boy had endeared themselves to most of the grounds crew and maintenance staff, and the dad hung out with them as if he were one of them. Within this organization, the dad had found his people. They had adopted the boy, given the boy the run of the place. In the process, the crew had discovered the joy of watching the Wiffle ball games the dad and boy played, and many made it a point to watch these games while they worked, always cheering for the boy, of course.

The dad initially set up the game in the right-field corner of the stadium, using the corner as the center-field walls of the Wiffle ball field. The first time he did this, all he could find for a home plate was a towel and a trash can to stand in for the tree. This setup lacked the charm of his home field, there was no shed to use as the triple, but it was still a lot of fun. There was not much for the boy to do away from home, so, at least initially, the pair played Wiffle ball a couple of times a day.

At first, only a few of the staff watched and then only for a minute or two as they went about their business. However, the more Wiffle ball the dad and boy played, the more they were noticed. Over the next couple of days, as more of the facility staff tuned in to watch and stayed longer, it became an event not to be missed among the crew.

On day three, when they showed up to play, the crew had pulled a portable backstop down into the right-field corner and placed a large cardboard tube at home plate to stand in for the tree.

Now the two old men sat perfectly still on the long wooden bench in the home field dugout, where only one person had noticed them. They sat feet in front, perfectly still, bellies out, arms crossed, with their backs against the wall, as they had their entire managerial careers.

Both despised that management was pulling this stunt and what it did to the game. To these old men, baseball was the most religious of events. It deserved to be treated with the utmost respect, and putting that joke of a man on the team was a blasphemy to the purity and history of the sport.

They were required to allow it, but they didn't have to like it, and certainly weren't going to do anything to help. But both men wanted the paycheck and loved the lifestyle, and while managers are sometimes fired midseason, they never quit. Besides, this team stunk, and it was only going to be for one at bat.

They sat in silence for quite a while, not sure what to think about what they were watching. These men were lifelong friends and had a shorthand when they talked about the game. Finally, they did:

"Nice curve." This meant: "Wow, did you see the break on that thing?"

"Yep." This meant: "Yikes! That was three or four feet."

"Slider?" This meant: "Holy cow, look, he can curve it in both directions."

"Yep." This meant: "Is that even possible? Amazing!"

It was an accident that they were in the dugout at that day and time. They did not wear the team uniform but rather the bright shirts and baggy pants that old men wear when they play golf. They were on their way to play golf and stopped at the stadium to pick up a pair of sunglasses and stumbled upon this event happening in the right-field corner. But managers will watch any and all baseball, and they sat down to take a look.

"Hit that good!" This meant: "Wow, he hit that home run a long way."

"Curve moves." This meant: "He's got a great curveball!"

"Damn!" This meant: "Dang! They are good at this."

They watched, going back and forth like this with a one comment every five minutes or so, with these vague, one-word answers spaced equally apart. Finally, one of them said:

"What do you think?" This meant: "I think we can make use of this."

"Yep?" This meant: "Nothing else has worked why not?"

"Think so!" This meant: "I agree."

"His kid?" This meant: "The guy has a kid?"

"Think so!" This meant: "Yep."

The boy thrived in this environment and had become much more animated and willing to interact with others. The fenced world in his backyard had become so familiar that he was bored with it. He needed to get out and see the world a bit, and this new world, while also fenced and protected, was full of marvelous things that were new to him, so he found it exciting.

As they played, his concern for the dark shadows grew. They looked at him too hard, so he studied them during breaks in the game. The shadows never moved, but their heads would often vibrate in a curious way that was new to the boy. Over time these figures warmed, and the edges softened, and that was odd as well. "They are up to something," thought the boy.

The oldest man on the grounds crew was in his late sixties. He had been mowing the field for the organization for twenty-five years. Considered excellent at his job, the old man knew the tricks of mowing the patterns that looked so great from the stands or on TV. As the "old guy," he had also become a mascot for the team and the person in charge of deciding when the field needed to be mowed, fed, and watered.

He took a shine to the boy before the rest of the crew. He discovered the boy sitting in the dirt box wagon one day as he sat down to mow and quickly realized that the boy liked to ride behind the mower. The boy would alternate between drawing in the dirt and hanging over the back of the wagon, face down, watching the endless blades of freshly cut grass pass by in front of his face. Mowing the entire surface took about two hours, so the first time they did this, the old man was continually looking back to check on the boy. The old man had no idea why the boy liked to ride behind him in the wagon while he mowed, but it seemed harmless enough.

The others called him "old man." He was the one that shortened grass, and of all the white shadows, he was the one that interested the boy the most. The boy was convinced that this man had the sight as well, although he didn't seem to know that he did. When the old man's face approached him, it did not swell in size, and his features did not distort like the others. The boy could see his skin without the patterns or textures, and his colors were soft and warm. The boy knew the old man could be trusted and that he understood, even if he didn't realize it.

The boy was aware of his differences and that he felt

trapped because he could see how others acted. He lived in a constant state of being hyperaware of everything that was happening around him. It was his normal state. He could listen to the sounds of everyone's clothing, of individual leaves rustling in a tree, or all conversations happening in a crowded room. He could never step away or turn off this massive load of useless input, so it dominated him always. He looked at the world through a fish-eye lens. This prevented him from isolating the smaller bits of information that he wanted to focus on, like a person's face or an individual voice.

The boy desperately wanted to be able to communicate his desires, but could not. Occasionally, he would stumble upon situations or things that would overwhelm his mind. On these occasions, something like a hole would open in his head that he could look through and that would allow him to focus on a single thought. He could see to the end of the tunnel, during that time, and feel himself moving toward the end. Ironically, the best way he had found to get relief was to watch the light flickering off water or as it traveled through the leaves. He also found that by rapidly flapping his hand and looking closely at the spaces between his fingers, he could gain the same therapeutic relief. Some vibrations or sounds helped, like static, running water, or a stadium full of people. If he did or experienced any of these things, he could get hours of calm.

The vibrations of the mower at the ballpark were different than the ones at home. The mower's sheer power caused tiny bits of grass to fly out and up and flicker in a cloud above the ground before settling down onto the field. This kaleidoscopic cloud of grass instantly provoked a unique hyperattentive trance, and it allowed him to occupy the busy part of his mind. It opened an iris, enabling him to ignore the other things happening around him and let him think about the things he wanted to. To the boy, it was like waking up at the end of a twenty-hour sleep.

BATTING COACH

Without the safety of the backyard there was little for the boy to do on his own during this time so the dad and his boy played Wiffle ball a couple of times each day. When father and son arrived for Wiffle ball later that same day, they were surprised to find the batting coach and a player waiting for them, all dressed up in team uniforms. The dad hesitated at first and wondered if they had got the schedule wrong.

The boy froze, his eyes narrowed, head pounding—he was afraid, terrified of this new presence. As it approached, he slowly dropped his forehead, eyes up, fixed on the dark fragments walking toward him. This presence was full of anger and hate, eyes black pits of fire. The boy drifted behind his dad. He moved away from it, out toward the place they played Wiffle ball, and away from this approaching ball of hate.

The batting coach walked up. Without introductions or even asking the boy's name, he demanded, "We want the boy to throw some curveballs to hotshot here, so let's get on that."

"Why?" replied the puzzled dad.

"Skipper thought it might help, hotshot can't hit curveballs. Come on, let's go, hurry up!"

The boy was already standing at the spot where they pitched from, forty-two feet away from home plate, waiting for his dad to grab a bat. Already annoyed with this arrogant man, the dad went out to his boy.

"Wait—we want the boy to pitch, stay off the field. Go sit down and stay out of the way," barked the batting coach.

Angered, the dad ignored the coach and continued walking out to his boy. He went to one knee to talk directly to his face. "They want you to pitch to this player. Can you try that for me?" The boy's flickering hand stopped moving, indicating a reluctance for this plan. The boy remembered all the times other people, family and friends, who tried to play in their game over the years. Outsiders to their game were always terrible, and the boy knew this man would wreck it.

The boy looked at the flurry of hate making noises at him from behind the backstop. He didn't like his presence. The coach yelled out, "Just tell him to throw the curve ball, dammit," followed by a whispered, "Jesus Christ, how hard can that be?"

At this, the dad of the boy went into full Papa Bear mode, turned to the coach, pointed his finger at him, and said in a calm but stern voice, "Hey! Shut up." He held the point for several seconds to stare the coach down, then purposely took his time before going back to the boy.

The boy tried to see around his dad and studied the presence as fragments of its skin shifted in violent spasms. Its blackness glowed like embers.

Every person working near the field saw this exchange and knew something big was happening. This coach was mean to everyone, no one had ever stood up to him, and certainly nobody told him to shut up. The crew all knew the coach was about to boil over. They drifted closer to get a better look at the action.

"They think it would help this man if you could teach him how to hit one of your great curveballs. Can you teach him how to do that?" the dad said quietly. "Can you pitch to him for a while? We can still play our game after, just you and I. Can you try that?"

With that, the boy's hand began to flicker, and the dad stood up and moved behind him. "OK, then. They want you to throw him curveballs. Can you throw him one?" The boy looked at the batter as if he was about to pitch but didn't do anything more, and his flicker hand went still. The dad realized right away the problem and called to the player. "You need a Wiffle ball bat."

The player turned to the coach. The coach was fuming by this point and yelled angrily: "This is the major leagues, and we use wood bats at this level," in the snottiest possible of tones.

"And while we're at it, you guys get over here and move the plate back the right distance. This is really stupid, goddammit. And get that tube out of there. What's it there for anyway? C'mon."

Whenever there is any kind of practice, there are several members of the grounds crew or facility staff there to take care of things that come up in the course of training. Instantly several of these guys sprang into action and started taking care of the coach's requests. In seconds, someone had a tape measure and moved the home plate to the MLB pitching distance of 60'6", while others removed the tube and slid the backstop back.

The dad watched the crew follow orders. Then, the dad and his boy started walking off the field without even a look at each other. This was an action that sent the batting coach into a rage.

"God dammit, where do you think you're going to, get back here! You don't walk out on me, this is the major leagues, at least try and act like it—"

Instantly the dad sprang into the coach's face.

"No, this is a Wiffle ball game, and you don't know a damn thing about it, so shut up and get out of our faces. We can go play this game in the street and be very happy. We don't need this field or you yelling at us to do it—"

The boy stepped away as the man's fragments swelled in size and stood erect like glowing blades of jagged glass. Its skin crackled and eyes shrunk to tiny dots of boiling fire as it looked at his dad.

The coach started to counterpunch, furious and red faced at the insolence. The dad cut him off, topping him loudly:

"What's my boy's name?"

The angry question stunned the coach, and he recoiled. The facility staff all started bowing their heads, trying not to be noticed in the background, but they loved every second of it.

"What's my boy's name?" the dad shouted again, even louder, stopping the coach entirely. "What's that player's name? Did you bother to introduce them, you idiot, did you even bother to say please and thank you?"

Then, in the best of baseball traditions, the dad got face to face with the coach, close enough to smell his breath.

"My boy does not like you. He is ten years old, he is autistic, mute, and he doesn't like you, and neither do I. If you want him to do this, then you get off the field and don't come back until I say so, and when you do—know his name."

The boy relaxed as he watched the anger soften and hatred fade. The man looked directly at him. As he did, the boy could see his eyes widen, his skin glow warm. The darkness faded, and with it, the boy's concern.

He watched as the man walked away until he reached the dugout. Another black shadow was waiting for him, and from a distance, the boy could see the man glow with hate and rage once again.

The coach turned and angrily walked back to the dugout. He was swearing up a storm when he noticed the team's manager sitting there, and stopped in his tracks. The manager had been sitting in the dugout unseen, and smiled at him.

"He sure kicked your ass!" After a pause, he continued on: "Shake it off, coach, he'll be gone tomorrow."

From his hiding place, the manager watched as the crew restored the Wiffle field, and the dad led the boy over to meet the player. They shook hands, and the boy went back out to the pitcher's spot. The dad handed the player a Wiffle bat, and then the boy threw curves at him for at least half an hour.

After the hitting lesson ended, the manager walked out to talk to the dad. It had been seven days and five games since the dad joined the team, and the manager had not said a word to him. Finally, the manager finally spoke. "Hey, the office tells me I have to bat you tomorrow, so do whatever it is you do to get ready, OK? Probably in the eighth.

Your boy has a pretty great curve!" With that, he walked away, not looking for further talk.

CATCHERS

By the next morning, the video of the dad yelling at the batting coach had already been shown on every sports show in America, and millions of people had seen it. Combined with the announcement that he was going to bat that day; the box office was selling tickets at a rate not seen in five years.

As far as the team was concerned, the plan had worked better than perfect. The attendance at the first two games was up a lot. Eighteen thousand extra tickets were sold for the first game, and twenty-three thousand for the second one. Attendance at the next three games was also much higher, but the public started complaining that the dad wasn't batting. As predicted, the numbers began to drop. But the fans that did show up were having a much better time.

The team started trying out lots of new ideas. Concessions started selling a whole new menu of cheaply priced items. The "Bowlegged Tiger Meal," a hot dog and a drink for a dollar fifty, was a big hit, as were the fifty-cent bottled water and two-dollar beer.

The dad took part in all the events the team planned to make the park more fun. First, it was a "Fat Man" contest where they put photos of chubby fans who volunteered on the scoreboard, and people voted for the one who looked most like the dad. And they followed the same format for "Best Bald Head" discount day, and "Worst Haircut Day," all of which he got to help judge. "Bug-Eyed Glasses Day" was pretty fun too. For him, the most fun was "Big Head Bobblehead Day," where the team

gave away bobblehead dolls that were supposed to be caricatures of him. The funny part was the little dolls didn't seem like
caricatures; he actually looked like a distorted bobblehead.

Overall, he was having a lot of fun interacting with fans.
The players and coaches mostly ignored him or made no effort
to interact with him. He quickly realized this was a great solution because he knew that he didn't belong either. That allowed
him to not have to try to act like them; he could just be himself.

He took batting practice before the other players arrived
or after they had left. The coaches were so disinterested in him
that they didn't even bother to watch. In their minds, and his
too, it was a foregone conclusion that he would strike out and
then immediately go away. So far, only the batting practice
pitcher and himself knew that he had yet to hit the ball in fair
territory.

The medical and training staff treated him the same way
they did all the players—like a king. He had never had a chiropractic session or massage in his life, but since he signed, he had
done it at least once every day, and he was feeling pretty fantastic.

During the games, he got to wear a uniform, and his name
was announced just like all the other players. He sat at the far
end of the dugout and tried to stay out of the way. To kill
time, he talked with the security guard, dugout staff, or the odd
player who forgot who he was and accidentally said something
to him. But mostly, he watched the game and marveled over the
speed, grace, and power of these gifted young men. He loved sitting so close to the action. It allowed him to witness the tiny
adjustments and conversations that happened during a Major
League game.

He had always admired them, but getting the opportunity to watch Major League catchers from this distance was his
biggest joy. He knew they were studs, but until he saw them
up close, he had no idea how tough and full of pride these men
were.

Catching requires the precision and nimble dexterity of

a surgeon, using hands brutalized repeatedly by foul tips and pitched balls bouncing off them for months on end. Imagine spending two to three hours crouching deeply in the hot sun, dressed in thick pads, and getting hit in the hands, arms, or groin with a baseball traveling at more than 90 mph, fifteen to twenty times a game.

The antelopes that graze the outfield, or the jackrabbits that wait around on the infield, typically return to the dugout daisy fresh. They exert themselves for just a play or two each inning. In contrast, catchers return to the dugout drained from the maximum physical and mental effort expended on every single pitch. They are both the plow horse and the brains of the team in a job that requires nonstop effort.

Covered in dirt and drenched in sweat, they sit on the bench between innings, hoping they don't have to bat so their knees have time to stop twitching and hands stop shaking so that they can do it again three outs later. And while you might hear other players complain or protest about the inhumanity of small injustices, you will never hear a catcher complain about anything.

THE BOSS PROBLEM

The dad was supposed to bat during tonight's game and he was extremely nervous about it. The last thing he wanted to think about was issues related to work. But, it was still morning and the boss had already called several times and was now calling again. He tried to ignore these calls but was torn because his boss had always treated him well so gave in and decided to answer.

"Yes, I have morning practice in five minutes, but we can talk for a bit, how can I help?"

While he was gone, it was agreed that his boss would step in and be in charge of checking tools in and out. Apparently, the boss had been having problems was finding a tool and needed the dad to help him locate it. "Well boss, I know, I'm frustrated too! but you told me it was OK for me to do this and it's not even been a week yet. Besides, I'll be home in the morning... Yep, I'll get released tonight after the game and will be home first thing," said the dad with great certainty.

"Just relax—I can give you turn-by-turn instructions and talk you right to where it is."

The dad listened intently as the voice on the other end of the line spoke. "Yes, I can tell you right where it is, no problem."

The dad resolved to be patient and helpful because this man had been his boss for twenty years and had been a wonderful person to work for. The boss was always patient and kind, and the dad wanted to act that way now as well. "OK, start by standing in front of my desk, looking right at it. Are you doing that?... Good! Now, turn right."

He chuckled at the response. "What do you mean, which right, are you kidding?" There is only one right!" he cringed realizing he did not sound patient.

But the voice continued with this odd line of questioning. "Yes, the one on the right," blurted the dad one more time.

The dad was now very upset at himself ... he wasn't being patient at all. Trying to recover the dad said, "Right, I mean correct, yes."

Flustered, he decided to start again, but before he could the boss had said something that sounded way off. "No, that's not right the spot, go back to my desk, and let's start over, OK?" he said trying to stay calm.

"Are you ready? OK, now stand so that you are in front of my desk, facing it."

The dad could hear some sort of a struggling but no audible reply. Then he did, "What? No! Not on it," he said with a hysterical blurt of laughter.

"No, I'm sorry, I shouldn't laugh. But be careful and get down off the desk and stand in front of it, ok boss? Yep, I'll wait."

The dad waited and tried not to laugh out loud as the boss found his way off the desk. As he did it occurred to him that one of the most frustrating things about being in the major leagues was how lost he felt in this strange new land of baseball. He didn't know where anything was or how it worked or even what he needed to do. It occurred to the dad that this must be how the boss was feeling as he made his way down the dark, narrow hallways of the tool cage. It angered him a bit that without realizing it, he had started treating his boss the way the people in this world treated him. Finally, it sounded like the boss was ready to go and hearing a positive response the dad started one more time.

"Good, you there? Are you looking at the desk?"

"What? What do you mean, which desk? There is only one desk." The dad giggled loudly at the absurdity of the question, thinking the boss must be playing, trying to trick him. "Boss, are you in the tool cage? . . . You're not?... Where are you?"

The dad laughed loudly thinking he now understood the problem. "Boss, all the tools are in the tool crib—you need to look there."

"Well, can you call me back when you're in the tool crib? OK, I'll be standing by."

As he listened to his boss's questions, he heard an unasked question far more revealing of the problems the boss was having than finding the correct tool. The boss didn't seem right at all, he seemed loopy and off, but since he would be home in the morning he knew seeing him then would give him a far better understanding of what was going on.

CLUB HOUSE

For not a single second had the dad of the boy felt like he belonged in the major leagues, and in no place was that clearer than when he was in the locker room. He had landed on his own alien world when he walked into this room and felt like an insignificant life form compared to the creatures in front of him. Most people go about their everyday lives surrounded by others who are more or less like themselves. The average person will go to a beach and walk around shirtless because they are surrounded by a collection of people like them, the skinny, thin, and scrawny, mixing with chubby, fleshy, and stout. In that environment, you are what you are because everyone else is that way too: imperfect.

Put that same average Joe on a beach full of supermodels or athletes, and they get self-conscious pretty quick. The differences between the physical characteristics of a professional athlete and an average person are vast. The professional athletes in this room were all young, strong, athletic, and beautiful, and many had no qualms about walking around completely nude. Nudity is binary. You like it, or you don't. Some men went about the business of changing quickly, while others seemed to walk around oblivious to the fact that they were nude.

On the other hand, the dad had not changed his clothes in front of anybody with the lights on in twenty-five years. The idea of being nude in a room with thirty-five other people . . . "No, that isn't going to happen!" he said to himself. He was proud to be a big-headed, bowlegged old man with varicose veins, a potbelly, and weird chest hair, but damned if he was going to change in front of mixed company while on TV.

When you see a locker room interview on TV, the image zooms in, from the chest up, on the person being interviewed. When you watch a TV interview from across the room, the person being interviewed is wearing little, if anything. In every locker room, there seems to be a reporter or two who is a woman. If you are a bowl of jelly, it's terrible enough changing in a room full of the perfect bodies of young male athletes. You can call him a fuddy-duddy, but the dad could not wrap his mind around taking his clothes off in front of a young, attractive female, especially while on TV!

Beyond that, this was just not a world he understood. All the men in this room had spent years learning the intimacies of baseball. After thousands of hours of lifting, stretching, and training their bodies, they were finely tuned to play the sport. Their physique reflected the advantages of being the focus of the best trainers, masseuses, and dietitians in the world. And now their bodies were perfectly developed for the sport in general, and the position they played in particular.

They were young, tall, solidly built men with obvious muscle. They had become part of the machine and rituals of a Major League locker room and the greater major leagues. They all knew the protocols, the how and whys, the unspoken rules, and shortcuts. These men were carefully selected from all over the country, from among the best of the best of their communities, regions, and the nation—no, the world.

It is assumed that by the time a player reaches a Major League locker room, they have had the experiences needed to understand what to do. They understand expectations, relationships, and the jobs of everybody they might meet. These men are under a state of constant evaluation. Many sets of eyes watch every flex, grip, and step they take, and they are carefully monitored, evaluated, and then compared to 150 years of baseball history. Perhaps no other occupation in the world is as carefully scrutinized as that of a Major League Baseball player.

Before now, nobody ever cared about how the dad felt or

what he might need. In the world he came from, he could break a leg, and nobody would notice for a week. In contrast, his first time in the locker room, a trainer walked up to him and asked him out of the blue:

"Do you need to be taped?"

At the time, he was tying his shoes and had no idea who this person was or why he was talking to him.

"No, thanks, I'll just tie them," he said.

Athletic trainers work intimately with the players on an MLB team and focus on keeping the players on the field by trying to prevent, diagnose, and treat muscle and bone injuries and illnesses. They apply tape, bandages, and braces, as well as provide first-aid care. They are incredibly essential servants to the players and are widely respected members of the team community.

"OK—is there anything else you have concerns about?" the trainer asked next.

He did not understand at all who this person was or what his job was. He looked down at his shoes and said, "I kind of wish these glowed in the dark!"

THE DIFFERENCES

They could not have come from more different worlds. One was young, pretty, tall, and slim. She attended a world-class university where she was an elite athlete and became a well-educated young woman who would later marry a wealthy man. In contrast, the other woman came from the world of country music, horses, leather, and rodeo. She married a simple man of labor with lots of emotional and physical challenges. Somehow, these two different women discovered a friendship in their differences, and in the past five days, the mom of the boy and the mother of twin girls had become good friends.

There are many types of people that make up the population of players' wives and girlfriends. Many understand how lucky they are to have married into the wealth of Major League Baseball and go about their lives treating others well. Other wives think of themselves as royalty and handle the newer, less pretty wives, or the wives of less established players, like peasants. But all the wives and girlfriends on this team respected the assistant general manager's wife. So when the mom of the boy appeared with her, they treated her respectfully as well.

The pair attended all the games together with their children, and both understood the significance of this particular game and how it would affect the fate of their friendship. After her husband batted tonight, one woman's husband would be cut from the team, and they would no longer have a built-in reason to be friends.

The team was still awful, but on this night, they seemed

inspired and played well, and the sellout crowd was loving it. In the third inning the right fielder, who had a reputation for not being able to hit a curveball, hit one over the wall in left field for a three-run home run. Three innings later, he doubled off that same wall to bring in two more runs, again off a curveball.

The dad had spent the first six innings in the clubhouse, preferring to stay away from the chaos of the game and the glare of his teammates. At the end of the sixth, he took a few halfhearted practice swings and started to wander around nervously. At the end of the seventh, the batboy appeared and gave him a message from the manager. "He says you're leading off when we bat in the eighth."

The dad had thought of nothing but this for the last week and was ready for it to all be over. He was looking forward to going home, going back to work, and playing in the backyard with his boy.

He decided he had better pee and went to take care of the issue. As he passed a mirror, he saw himself for the first time in a Major League Baseball uniform. He turned and studied the misfit looking back at him. "Damn," he said, shaking his head, "how is this possible?" After a long exhale, he slumped to the bathroom floor, back against the door, and flipped off the light. Disappointed to discover that these team-issued shoes did not glow in the dark, he shut his eyes and listened as the world marched on without him.

Through the door, he could hear the crowd and the muffled sounds of the loudspeaker. Finally, in the distance, he could pick out the music indicating the end of the first half of the eighth inning. Seven warm-up pitches were now all that stood between him and the sound of that same loudspeaker calling him to bat. Through the door, he heard the shuffling sounds of the batboy trying to find him, and in the distance, the music stopped.

He flipped the switch, and the first thing he saw were the bright-orange shoes that players were wearing for tonight's game. "Don't fail me now," he thought. Head down, he followed his cleats as they marched him through the clubhouse and into the dugout. Oblivious to his teammates, he found the steps leading to the field. He proceeded quickly to the batter's box, arriving just as they announced his name.

In the wives' section, he found his wife's nervous face and then his son's frozen stare looking back at him. He stepped into the box and then looked out at the pitcher. From behind him, the umpire chirped, "Play ball." And the pitcher immediately delivered a fastball for a strike.

He instantly felt dizzy and nauseated. Flashes of light danced in front of his eyes, so he backed out of the box and bent down, fighting the urge to puke. This action provided some relief, so he grabbed a handful of dirt, rubbed his hands together, and got back in the batter's box. To the outsider, these actions appeared normal, as many players go through a similar routine between pitches.

Again, he looked out at the pitcher, and his field of vision was a blur of fragments moving and shifting in front of him. He was fighting to clear them when again the pitcher fired another fastball for a strike. Once more, he backed out, this time gagging, knowing that if he puked, it would be in front of fifty-five thousand people and a TV audience.

As he fought the impulse, he could feel himself starting to faint. The spinning intensified; his vision darkened. The flashes became kaleidoscopic, moving hypnotically wherever he looked. His knees weakened, so he squeezed his eyes tightly shut and prayed, "Just twenty seconds, God. Please just give me twenty seconds more." Suddenly he felt stable, so he grabbed some more dirt, jumped back in the batter's box, and looked out at the pitcher through the spinning patterns one last time.

FAINT

His head was down, and he desperately tried to concentrate on just putting one foot in front of the other until he could reach home plate. His vision was failing, and the tunnel of light was growing smaller with each step he took. Fainting was inevitable, it was just a matter of when. It took all his effort to stay lucid until he stepped on home plate. Somehow, he made it and then managed to get to the steps of the dugout. He stumbled his way up the hall and through the bathroom door. He locked the door before falling to his knees on the bathroom floor. He vomited, then rolled onto his back in the pool of vomit the room spinning in a blur of spots until it grew dark.

The fluorescent ceiling lights were the first things he saw when he woke up. He watched these lights as they appeared to multiply and bend like noodles, his mind fighting to find the reality he knew he must restore. He had no idea how long he had been lying there, but once awake, he did not move for a very long time. Instead, he closed his eyes and listened to the sounds of his breathing and of his heart thundering in his chest.

Gradually he became aware of sounds on the other side of the door, and slowly the sounds of distinct voices emerged from the chaos. His heart calmed, and his eyes cleared again. He sat up, then stood, then leaned against the sink and made sure he had found his feet before he raised his head. When he did, he saw his face in the mirror. His eyes red, he had the look of a man who had just slept in a pool of his own vomit. He washed his face, took off the jersey and used it to quickly clean the mess on the floor, then rinsed the vomit from it in the sink. As he squeezed the last of the water from it, there was a knock at the door.

He made his way to the chair in front of his locker, wearing a T-shirt and what still remained of his uniform when a crowd of reporters came toward him. The other players knew this drill and drifted away and pretended not to listen. Without any pleasantries, the reporters surrounded him and began a barrage of questions.

"Are you aware that you now hold the record for the oldest rookie ever to hit a home run in his first at bat?"

"No, I'm not. I mean I wasn't—"

"It must be exhilarating, hitting a home run on your first at bat. What were you thinking?"

"What do you mean?"

"Can you take us through your at bat? What were you thinking? Did you have a plan?"

"Well, yeah. My first thought was to not get killed."

After a few awkward chuckles from within the group, another voice asked, "Anything else?"

"Sure, ahhh. Enjoy the moment, I guess . . . just try not to embarrass myself too badly. My son was watching."

"You took the first two pitches. Why?"

He tried to locate the face this question came from but never did, so again he took his time and answered to the center mass of the group. "I've been watching baseball for . . . since I was a boy. I'm a huge fan of the game, and I've always wanted to see what a pitched ball from a Major League pitcher looked like."

"Looked like?"

"Ya, up close, from the batter's box, to really see it, so . . . I had decided . . . I planned that no matter what, I was gonna take the first two pitches," he said, looking around again to find the face that asked the question.

"Why not swing at everything, give yourself a better chance of hitting something?"

He turned toward the question and looked up, "I had no chance of hitting anything—these guys are gods. I'm just . . . I had no illusions that I would hit anything. I mean, what are the odds?"

"But you did, how do you explain that you did?"

"I got lucky, he got unlucky, I can't explain it. I've never even played high school ball, he's a real Major League pitcher, a good one . . . hell a great one?" He then paused, and it hit him that every single person in the room was looking at him.

"I got no chance to hit him or anybody else, so I had decided that what I could get out of this is the memory of what a real pitch looked like up close. I figured that would take two pitches."

From directly in front of him, a faced blurted, "So what was it like?"

He shook his head in amazement. "It was like a bomb exploding right next to me!"

"A bomb?"

"Ya—the power. The power. It feels like something has exploded in front of you as it crosses the plate," he said in awe. "I had no idea a human could do that with a baseball. Watching on TV, you have no idea what these guys can do."

"Go on."

"I mean, it was terrifying, and it was perfect all at the same time. The sound of it . . . I wasn't expecting the sound."

The reporters began to lean in, as this was not the typical interview full of clichés and thoughtless sound bites.

"The sound?"

"You don't hear the sound a baseball makes when you sit in the stands or watch on TV or even in the dugout."

"What did it sound like?"

He shut his eyes and then, as if retelling a religious happening: "It's like *whoosh* on steroids, like a lightsaber swing and miss. It's terrifying and beautiful at the same time. It vibrates your soul—"

A few of the players had stopped pretending not to listen and gathered on the outer ring, watching with the reporters. He nodded his head toward the players in the back and went on.

"It made the hairs stand up on my arms, the back of my neck, like you're in the presence of gods! I can still feel it." The room became hushed.

One of the reporters sarcastically broke the moment. "In the presence of gods? Wow! Are you kidding? It's not every day we hear a player offer such praise of other players."

Faster now, and feeling a little foolish, he said, "I'm not a player, I fetch parts in a tool crib for a living. A week ago I was on my couch. I'm just a schlub."

"A schlub?"

He chuckled then. "Yeah. A normal guy—a fat guy, an ugly guy, a schlub. I'm nobody, like everyone else. It's different for us than for these guys. They have prepared their whole lives to be here, to them this is all normal. I won a raffle. To me, this is all amazing."

"During your at bat, you seemed pretty calm out there, stepping out of the box, scooping up dirt. Were you?"

"No, I thought I was gonna puke, I was trying not to puke . . . or faint. Both, I guess."

"You started walking before home plate. Were you trying to show up the pitcher?"

"No! Seriously, I was trying not to faint. I remember getting to third base, and when I looked toward home, everything started getting dark. My knees started to buckle; walking was all I had left."

"Are you sick?"

"No. Think about it, this is a pretty big night for me. Who expected this? I didn't."

"So, when you saw the ball go out—that had to be very surreal—what were your thoughts?"

"I didn't see it." He shook his head in regret. He was appalled at the faint aftertaste of vomit that has suddenly appeared in his mouth.

"You didn't see your home run?

"No, it happened too fast. I saw the first-base umpire doing the home-run signal. I never did locate the ball. Where did it go?"

"You hit it over the left-field wall into the bullpen." Someone handed him the baseball, and he stood up to take it. Someone had already written his name, the date, place, and in big letters, all caps, "1ST MAJOR LEAGUE HOME RUN!" on it.

"Wow." He looked at the ball. "That's unbelievable. This whole thing—unbelievable."

"When do you think you will bat again?"

He snapped out of his trance and perked up. "Tomorrow, in the backyard, with my son." He smiled. "I'm going home in the morning."

There was a puzzling reaction from the reporters in the room that was equal parts surprise and curiosity.

"Are you quitting?"

"No, this was just a stunt, and it's over now. It was fun, but they told me they were releasing me." He then sat down to study his new ball. "Thanks, guys."

As he sat down, many eyebrows lifted, and the reporters looked around to read the faces of their peers in the room. It was clear to all that he was the only one that did not understand that this was not the end of the story.

THE PAYCHECK

The reporters eventually drifted away, and at last, he was left alone. He leaned forward in his chair, looked down at his shoes, and smiled. He held his gaze there for several long seconds, then, still soaked in sweat and smelling of vomit, he leaned back in the posture of an exhausted man.

The hand on his shoulder snapped him to attention, and a voice said, "You have to set up auto-deposit. Can you do that for me?" He looked up, and a man he did not know shoved an envelope into his hand. "It sure would help, OK, buddy? That's one week's pay. "

He sat up a bit and looked down at the envelope, then slid a finger under the seal and slowly ripped it open. He saw it contained a check and used his fingers to push open the walls of the envelope. Without removing it, he glanced inside and saw $16,278.12 peeking back at him. He started to cry.

He quickly remembered where he was and gathered himself when he noticed a pair of shoes in front of him. He looked up into the face of the batting coach from yesterday and immediately stood up.

"Listen, I can be an ass. It works for me. It's what I've always been. I am sorry about that!" said the man in a tone that confirmed his analysis.

The dad stood up, trying to deduce where this might be going. "I would like Chad, your boy . . . that's his name, right, Chad?"

Concerned, the dad considered the question without answering.

"I would like Chad to throw a bit in the morning, let our third baseman try and hit a few of those fancy curves. Would that be OK? 9 a.m.?"

Disarmed at the request, the dad lowered his defenses. "Ah, well . . .we have to . . . you know they released me . . . we're going home in the morning."

At that, the coach quickly apologized, shook his hand, and forced a smile. Pointing at the dad's envelope, he said, "Those paychecks are pretty great, aren't they?" He turned away and moved off toward the door.

The dad watched the man go, and from the same direction came another, the assistant GM, the husband of his wife's new best friend, was walking toward him, hands in his pockets with a big smile on his face. He stopped and looking directly at the dad. "Exciting night!"

The two men stood there looking at each, and each smile grew a bit. "I see you got your paycheck?

So, what are your plans?" said the assistant GM with a goofy look on his face.

The dad started telling him the plans for getting an early start and leaving first thing in the morning to get back home.

"Actually," interrupted the man, "I just talked with your wife. She's out in the hall, waiting for you, with some friends. By the way, she says it would be OK if you stayed here with us another week. So, what do you say, wanna give this one more try?"

THE PARTY

As he left the clubhouse, the dad immediately saw his boy flicking his hand in his direction. Behind him stood his wife with a goofy smile on her face. He moved forward to hug his boy but was ambushed by the neighbor. The man's booming voice intercepted him and started an overwhelming sequence of questions. Knowing this would happen, the mom stepped back between them and hugged the dad, expertly turning him away from the neighbor and including the boy in the hug. "I invited a few friends," whispered the mom, and the dad looked out to see what appeared to be everybody from his hometown.

Looking down at her, her wide eyes so bright and pretty, he remembered why he had fallen in love with her all those years ago at Niagara Falls. He met his wife at Niagara Falls, of all places—in the city, not the falls. Actually, they met at a rodeo there when they were both in their early twenties. At the time, she was a barrel racer competing in a rodeo, he was just a lost soul wandering around the event to see what all the fuss was about.

She was a highly skilled rider who was ranked in the Canadian top twenty, and he happened to enter the viewing area as she started her race. She came in too fast around the first barrel, and the horse couldn't make the turn, so she wiped out in a cloud of dust, just ten feet in front of him. To him, it looked like the horse landed right on top of her; not understanding what he was seeing, and without thinking, he hopped the fence to help, only to get kicked in the head by her horse.

She, of course, was a seasoned rider and knew very well how to avoid injury, but nonetheless was charmed by the heroic efforts of this odd little man. She followed as security dragged his still-unconscious body out of the stadium and left him by a pile of manure. When he woke up, she was standing above him, arguing with the police as they wrote him a trespassing ticket for going onto the field.

She was taller than him, dressed in cowgirl style in jeans, a big buckle, boots, and sporting a knee-length ponytail. They married a few years later and had always lived in Michigan. In the time between then and now, she had made a life with him by making custom saddles and horse-related leather products in the family basement. She sold those products on the art fair and rodeo circuit throughout the Midwest.

Knowing she had found a knight in shining armor, a man willing to jump to her rescue at his own peril, was all she needed to know that he was the one. In the twenty years since, her brown hair had turned silver, but then, as now, they were always a physical mismatch, she athletic, outgoing, and pretty, and he, not.

For the mom, the really fun part of the night was introducing all her friends to the apartment. She waited outside the elevator door to greet it each time it brought a new load of people up to the party. As soon as they were all off the elevator, and door shut, she would make a big show of pressing the fob and watching her friends' reactions as the jukebox swung open. She would then giggle at their universal shock at the glittering world they saw inside the apartment.

There is a simplicity that is often lost in the way mankind records the actions of other men. Far too often, our historians glory at the deeds of our leaders, artists, and athletes, and universally ignore the acts of common men.

These were uncomplicated people who came from a simple way of life. They wore the uniforms of trades that plumb, paint, deliver, and drive, and do a thousand other things that go unnoticed by the world. Yet, they were the foundation holding up the weight of that world. The dad's people were average people, living simple lives of honest work for honest pay. They earned what they had, and shared what they made, wanting only to take care of their family and live in the company of friends.

The Bible called them "the salt of the earth," and Shakespeare referred to them as "mechanicals." The dad called them his family and friends, and it was normal for these people to have their parties in backyards, bars, and church basements using grills, kegs, and card tables. Tonight, they would play in a hidden palace reserved for kings, all because one of their own had accidentally done something that historians had noticed.

Eight hours from now, the morning sun would kiss crystal fixtures through golden sheets of lead and stain, revealing salty folk who played too long. The first to sleep would choose gilded beds or calfskin couches while the later spirits would tuck in on the luxury of handmade carpets.

The early risers that day were children. At first, they snuck and snickered, but then they bounced and banged. And soon, the room groaned with the crusty eyes of their moms and dads, all of whom were accustomed to wine and beer, but on had on this night indulged in house champagne.

The host of the party did not play that night because he had to practice in the morning. He rose before the children, snuck between the bodies strewn around the floor, and found the boy already waiting at the door.

WIFFLE BALL BATS

Wiffle ball bats are lightweight and made of sturdy yellow plastic. They are long and skinny. At its thickest point, a Wiffle ball bat is no more than 1.5 inches thick. It is tubular in shape, lacking the iconic tapering of a baseball bat.

Because of the bat's narrow dimensions, the hitter has to center the ball perfectly, and if they do, they are rewarded with a deep fly ball. If the hitter is the smallest fraction too high or low at the point of contact, they will pop up or ground out. While many Wiffle players can hit home runs, power has nothing to do with accomplishing that. Instead, hitting a Wiffle ball is totally about eye-hand coordination and proper form. Nothing else matters.

There are no degrees of success concerning hitting a Wiffle ball. It is a binary game; you either hit a home run or you do not. You must be perfect, so swinging hard or having height, weight, or muscles is irrelevant. Proper hitting form at the exact moment the ball hits the bat is essential. The batter must form a right angle with his hands, and the bat must meet the ball while it is in front of him. If the hitter allows the ball to get in on him, it is just not possible to hit a home run. The ball will glance off the bat, and swinging harder does not help.

When the dad and boy showed up to play Wiffle ball again that day, the dad was surprised to find the batting coach and three of the team's players waiting for them, all dressed up in team uniforms. The dad hesitated at the sight of more players and wondered what was going on. The boy, however, was intrigued and ran ahead of him toward the field.

The boy noticed the batting coach first, but also that he was different this time. The darkness was gone, and there was a serenity in its place. His colors were warm and patterns soft. Changes like these were quite unusual, so much so that the boy was eager to get close so he could study the metamorphosis.

Upon seeing the pair, one of the players jogged over. He knelt down in front of the boy, who stopped in front of him. "Hi, Chad. My name Lance and I would love to learn how to hit your curveball. Would you mind teaching me how to do that?"

Chad's hand flicked in response, and Lance looked up at the dad and stood back up. "That would be fine," said the dad, smiling and shaking hands with Lance.

With that, Lance bent back down to Chad and pointed to the other players. "Chad, the ugly guy out there is Greg—you already know him—but that other ugly guy is Raphael. He's not very good, and he really needs help," he said smiling up at the dad. "He plays shortstop, and he wants to learn too. Can you help him?"

And so, they played and played and played. Since the group only had the one bat and three Wiffle balls that the dad brought with them, the grounds crew eventually joined the players to field balls, and teams were formed quickly. The boundaries between professional and amateur disappeared as an ordered professional practice dissolved into a giggling group of kids playing Wiffle ball like in any backyard, anywhere, except this one was in the corner of a fifty-five-thousand-seat stadium.

The boy pitched for one team and the dad the other, and initially, it was about hitting a curveball. Quickly it dissolved into any pitch, any time, and boys just having fun. By the time they finished, the fifteen members of the field staff were either playing in the game or standing on the field cheering them on.

This was the happiest moment of the boy's life. The people with him now were there only to be with him, and they all wanted to be there. There was no discomfort or forced feelings or concerns—just comfort.

"What is this feeling?" he thought. Warmth and acceptance oozed from the skin of every participant. They became a vista of bright-orange figures dancing in a sea of vibrant blues and greens. It was the glee of people in a Henri Matisse painting: people dancing, a celebration of life and of being with each other. The boy had had never been included before, let alone the center of attention. These feelings were new to him, and while he could not express them on the outside, he was bubbling happily on the inside and wanted more of this.

The batting coach leaned on the backstop, watching this game for the better part of two hours, fighting every urge to interject, stop, or control the action that unfolded in front of him. This was especially true when his players were unable to hit the kid's pitches. Gradually, though, they started to make contact. Like Greg the day before, they quickly got the hang of it. He fought the urge to not let them do too much, because in his world of heavy bats, fast pitches, and hard swings, a player can actually take too much batting practice and injure himself. But there is no wear and tear in Wiffle ball because there is no weight, resistance, or stress when swinging. After thirty minutes, he realized there was no downside to just staying out of the way and letting them go.

SERIOUSLY?

I t was the seventh inning when the dad's cell phone rang. The manager instantly pointed at the hallway and angrily barked, "Get that thing out of here now!" The team had a strict no-phone policy during games so the dad was more than a little embarrassed as he left the dugout for the team locker room.

"Boss, it's the middle of a game, I can't talk right now."

But the boss sounded desperate so the dad made the mistake of asking, "OK, what can I do?"

He listened a few seconds then cut the boss off. "Seriously? --Why would you think that's OK? "

"I know you're the boss but what does moving the shelves accomplish, they're still shelves. They would just be in a different spot?" The dad listened a few seconds before continuing on. "Boss, but why not just move the part to the shelf?"

But that didn't seem to faze the boss at all and his suggestions we growing increasingly unbelievable. "Boss, it's the alphabet.... Yep the same one as always -- It's been the alphabet for a really long time, do we really need a new one?"

The dad was in a near panic because while he wanted to help his obviously distraught friend he did not want to get cut from the team for talking on the phone, "Why would you put that part there and no, it can't go in your car, or your boat. Just put everything back exactly in its place."

"Boss, please I gotta go ... but if you bend it, it's worthless - cutting it in pieces too!"

There is a loud crashing noise on the other end of the line.

"What was that noise, boss?"

Near tears, the dad switched off his phone and placed it on a shelf in his locker before sneaking head down back to his spot at the end of the bench.

FREAK SHOW

P.T. Barnum started his traveling "freak show" in 1835. The freaks of the show were people who had every imaginable physical misfortune and quite a few unimaginable ones as well. Many of these poor souls were horribly deformed. That reality made them unable to make a living any other way. Perhaps the most famous of Barnum's human attractions was a man named Charles Stratton. Mr. Stratton suffered from a condition that caused him to completely stop growing once he reached the age of six months. By the time he was a fully grown man at the age of eighteen, he had stood just twenty-five inches tall. "General Tom Thumb's" value to P.T. Barnum was his lifelong ability to sell tickets to a curious public, and he could do that only because he could never grow up.

Everyone knew that the dad's value to the team was time-sensitive and very limited. So far, the big-headed wonder had hit two home runs in a Minor League ballpark and one more in the majors. He would lose all value to his team the first time he did not hit a home run, and the Major League record for consecutive home runs at the start of a career was only three. Everyone expected that his next at bat would be his last. The front office's mandate was that he would not bat again until they returned home and could bat in front of a home crowd, and then not until the third or fourth game of the home stand.

But the team was in San Diego that night, and this was the first game of a five-game road trip to the West Coast. San Diego is a National League team, so there is no designated hitter in that league, and pitchers are routinely pinch hit for, especially in the later innings. This game was in extra innings, so the manager could care less about mandates. Since he had used up all his players, he had no other options.

The dad was oblivious to what was going on in the game. He sat at the end of the dugout, generally ignoring the action of the game, when the manager looked at him and said, "Grab a bat." The dad didn't think that there was the remotest possibility of him batting that night, so he failed to immediately respond, lost in the wonders of playing "rock, paper, scissors" with a security guard at the far end of the dugout. The manager glared at him until someone shook him and said: "You're up, you're up. C'mon, you're up."

He jumped to his feet and was immediately pushed onto the field as someone handed him a bat. So new was he to the game of baseball that he didn't even take a practice swing. He just marched to home plate, head down. As he stepped into the batter's box, the batboy caught up to him and handed him his helmet.

There were two on, with two outs, and the game was tied 7–7 in the top half of the sixteenth inning. There would be no long, drawn-out, tortured thought process leading up to this at bat—everything was happening too fast. Before the television announcers could say his name, he hit the first pitch over the wall in left field.

By that point, an estimated 217,000 games had been played in the history of Major League Baseball. The talking heads on the television that night agreed they had never seen or heard of anything close to what happened next, and no one knew how to handle this situation.

The television replays of what happened are now iconic, much like Gibson's home run or the George Brett pine-tar incident. The video of this incident shows the clearly shocked look on the dad's face as he hit the ball and watched it fly. Next, it shows him, like a toddler with a full load in his diapers, as he begins his bowlegged journey toward first base. But, the star of this video can be seen only if you look very closely at the small flutter in the area around his right ankle as his shoelace begins to untie.

About the same time as the ball goes over the fence, he gives a little hop and stumbles a bit. But, he recovers, and as he does, the shoelace goes into a full-on floppy mode, and begins to hunt its prey. Unaware of this predator, he approaches first base. He touches it and takes a few more steps before the shoelace then tangles fully. The lace slams him violently, jaw first, into the ground.

In those 217,000 games, lots of players have hurt themselves running the bases. Most are simply tagged out, and that's the end of that at bat. Many of those players trip for whatever reason, and most scramble back to a base, or are tagged out, ending the at bat. As far as anybody knows, no player in the history of Major League Baseball had ever hit a go-ahead, game-winning home run, and then tripped running the bases, knocking themselves out cold.

About the same year that P.T. Barnum invented the freak show in 1835, Abner Doubleday invented the game of baseball. In all the years, before this moment, the really freaky thing to consider is nobody had written a rule, invented a mechanism to help, or even check on, a player in this situation. So, he was left to lay there in limbo as chaos ensued around him on this beautiful night in San Diego.

For his run to count, he had to wake up, get up, and then run under his own power, all the way around the bases, making sure to touch all of them, including, and most important of all, home plate. Until he did, the game was in limbo, and this was still an active play. He could not be helped or assisted by his team in any way, and if someone did help him, he would be out, his run would not count, and the inning would end.

Ethics be damned! All hell broke loose as everybody started arguing about what to do. The trainers wanted to run on the field to help, as they obviously could not leave a medically distraught player without attention. But one trainer was physically restrained by the coaching staff who didn't want to give up a potential game-winning run. A couple of coaches and a trainer pushed and pulled at each other, locked in a dance, a desperate goal-line stand to keep the trainer off the field and away from the dad, serenaded by the old managers frantic yells to wake the sleeping hero. Meanwhile, a few feet away, the umpires conferenced about what to do, and every single soul in the stands stood in awe as they watched the freak show unfold before them.

Finally, the first baseman got on his knees and bent down close to the dad's face, and then rose to his feet. As he did, the entire stadium became silent as an empty church as everybody waited to hear what the town crier had to tell them. In a voice loud enough to reach every corner of the ballpark, the first baseman announced, "He's snoring. I think he's asleep!" With that proclamation, the crowd went wild.

This freak show went out in living color. Major sports shows interrupted their programming to show a live feed of the situation, broadcasting in vivid detail a painfully close image of the dad's drooling face as he lay sleeping, face down on the red infield dirt of what was then known as Jack Murphy Stadium while all America watched in awe.

Finally, at the ten-minute mark, as this chaos was reaching a crescendo, he opened his great big bug eyes on live TV and looked around like a confused toddler, wondering what in the world was going on. In private moments we've all seen people wake up looking disoriented, but this freak show was seen on nationwide TV. After a couple of cringe-worthy closeups, he sat up, wobbling like a drunken sailor. Lost in a stupor that made him oblivious to the reality that the whole world was watching, he adjusted his glasses and picked his nose for a painfully long time. Then, he tied his shoe, climbed to his feet, and still wobbly, slowly staggered around the bases.

A MASK

The dad had always assumed that his boss was educated and intelligent. Among the workers, it was known that he was, in fact, a college-educated man, and all assumed he was the smartest man in the room. A man of fifty-nine, he was clean-cut and well-groomed, projecting an organized, professorial air. He combined his position of power and conservative dress with always carrying a thick, serious-looking book or folded financial page. He typically selected from a variety of horn-rim spectacles, bow ties, and cardigan sweaters that he wore even in the summer.

The blue-collar workers in the company liked his calm, patient style of leadership and his fairness in dealing with the men he supervised. Workers in the shop believe it was the dad's system and rules used to organize and run the tool crib. In truth, it was the boss who, as a very young man, many years earlier, created a system that was still in use and passed it onto the dad.

The boss took a big chance when he hired the dad twenty years ago. The dad had little to offer the world and was confused by it, and it by him. His odd looks, habits, and social skills, combined with a rustic resume of questionable skills, menial jobs, and little personal accomplishment, did not make him an ideal candidate. He did not ask why, nor was the reason offered, for his hiring. However, real employment started a metamorphosis from grotesque misfit to a valued employee and gave him more than that a sense of place, purpose, and belonging within a community. As expertise and accomplishment awoke, so did a loyalty, well earned by the man who planted a seed in fertile ground and provided the time for it to bloom into a life of purpose.

In the last twenty years, the company doubled in size and then doubled again, and with it, the scope and content of the tool crib. The dad had taken his yearly vacation at this time every year with no ill effects on the company, so no one thought his absence would be a problem. It was just going to be a week, just like every year. Like every year, the boss, with his prior history of running the crib, decided that he would take over the dad's duties. On his way out the door, the dad's last words were, "Call me if you need help finding anything."

The dad was in the right-field corner near the access tunnel when the call came in from his boss.

"It's OK, I have time now, just got out of practice. How can I help?

The dad listened patiently for a while and then began to scrunch up his face a bit. Then, trying to speak clearly in his best imitation of his boss: "Boss, it's straightforward. Remember it's your system—everything has a place, everything goes in that place, every time?"

Before he could continue, he was cut off. Listening, he became concerned. Finally, he interrupted and began to talk as fast as he could:

"But boss that's not where that goes. You gotta follow the rules...if it's big, it is stored on the ground."

The dad listened intently to what the boss was telling him but became instantly upset at what he was hearing. "If you put it there—wait, how would you even get it there?" the boss had told the dad that he had somehow managed to put a large heavy part on top of the soft chain link ceiling of the tool gage. "But if you put it there—" As he started to speak the dad realized the impossibility of the bosses claims, "Is that even possible?"

"Boss just follow the rules...If it's big but small enough to lift, then it is stored on the bottom two shelves."

Again, the dad was interrupted so he stopped and listened intently. Finally, he had to interrupt," but that's too hard to remember, just use the system. . . . No, no, no! The little or light stuff is stored on the top three shelves. Put the small stuff in drawers, and tiny stuff in the slots in the drawers."

As he listened to this trusted voice, one previously of calm, reasoned authority, he realized it had been a costume masking a reality that was now exposing itself. His boss was not, or at least was no longer, the highly intelligent man of shop legend, but rather was operating on the fringe of a different reality.

"But, boss, everything already has a name. The guys will always request a tool by its name. If you take off the labels, no one will know what the part is, what it's used for, or where it goes so please don't do that—please!"

At this point, the dad shook his head non stop side to side as he listened to the delusional solutions on the other end of the line.

"Are you kidding?" Don't do that either. Really, don't do that—all the aisles already have names. A to C, E to F, G to J, and like that. It's right there on the ends of the shelves at eye level. . . . Yes, really! . . . Are you OK? . . . Boss how about you tell all the guys to keep the tools at their stations, and I'll pick them all up and put them back when I come back in a few days."

MOMMA MANDRILL

Travel is a big part of the experience for a Major League player, but it was all a new experience for the dad. His life was small, and his family did not do big things. They were happy and comfortable but settled for simple choices. He was twenty-five and she was twenty-four when they married. They had the boy the same month she turned twenty-eight, and now the boy was eleven years old. They always had jobs but never much money, so vacations had become fishing and camping trips to a local place, a KOA, or a trip to the water park. Travel meant a drive down to Coldwater, Michigan, where they would fish and stay at the Motel 6 just off the interstate. An expensive vacation to an exotic city was just not remotely a consideration.

But baseball teams travel all the time, and it is team policy that twice a year wives and children can travel with the team. Most wives want to travel to the more exciting or exotic cities. So, when the team went to San Diego, there was often a large contingent of wives and children traveling with them.

The team had organized a family visit to the San Diego Zoo. This zoo is in a gorgeous setting carved into beautiful Balboa Park in the heart of San Diego. In addition to its animals, the San Diego Zoo has a vast collection of botanical plants, a fantastic orchid garden, even a butterfly jungle. It is a geographically massive park with a broad assortment of animals, including panda bears and mandrills. It provides the animals with habitats that match their original homes. With so much to offer, there was a large group of team wives and children at the zoo that day.

One of the most challenging aspects of being the parent of an autistic child is the realization that your child will not fit in or be accepted. All parents protect their kids, and it is heartbreaking to see that when your child is different, other parents actually train their kids to stay away, as if it might be contagious, and the kids sometimes do this on their own. The parents of an autistic child understand that it takes a special person to embrace things they don't comprehend, to open up to and include the "different" members of their community. So far, the parents of the boy had met very few of these kinds of people.

It can be frustrating for the family of an autistic child because parents desperately want their child to be accepted by other kids. But some autistic kids require precise routines or rituals and can get very upset when a method is changed, even the slightest amount. These kids can become fixated on certain activities or objects or have incredibly fussy eating habits. Autistic children can also have odd-looking repetitive behaviors. Rocking, jumping, twirling, or hand-flapping are typical, and these actions can seem weird to those who do not understand what they are seeing.

Such was the case here. While his family loved him, the boy did not have friends. His mom worried about how he would do in the company of others, in a strange world full of new sights and sounds. This would be a day of new experiences at the zoo, and she was worried.

There are many degrees to autism. Some people with autism are intellectually limited, while others are quite brilliant. Other autistic people are fully functional and live productive, full lives, with most people not realizing they are on the spectrum. These people can have a family and make friends and live what is considered a normal life—they just have what others might call "quirks."

The boy was a flapper, and his hand-flapping had become a sort of mood ring that was an indication of what he was thinking. A fast flapping meant yes or that he was extremely excited.

The static state was constant slow flapping, and this said he was OK or that he was watching or listening. If, on the other hand, he completely stopped flapping, it meant no or that he was extremely interested in, or frightened by, something.

Mood rings were once considered real jewelry, and at the height of their popularity in 1975, these rings were expensive and were worn by the world's biggest stars. The idea behind a mood ring is that it is a biofeedback aid and reflects the cosmic vibrations or mood of the wearer by changing colors. Blue is an indication of sadness, while reds mean happy, and each color in between is attached to a specific mood. To many people mood rings were an odd fad because most people know what mood they are in, so the need for a ring seems trite. In spite of that, mood rings were hugely popular back them, even though scientifically and historically, they are regarded as a sham. Then again, the 1970s also brought massive popularity to the Pet Rock, Disco, and bell-bottom pants.

Some people believe that all things have an energy field or vibration that surrounds them. Many claim the ability to see these vibrations, and that they take the form of colors or patterns that shift or change, depending on the mood or purity of the person. People of the highest purity are incredibly rare. Among believers, these souls offer vibrations that are the most colorful, dynamic, and the purist whites and yellows.

Historically it is only the special ones, mystics, shamans, witch doctors, medicine men, and the sick or crazy among us, who can see these vibrations. Those coherent enough to articulate what they see teach us the best way to experience these energies is to look off to the side of the person whose "energy" you hope to see.

Animals, too, are known to have the ability to see things that normal humans cannot. For example, there is something not fully understood about the physiology of cats, reindeer, and some members of the ape family. Scientists have figured out that these animals can see far into the UV end of the spectrum, and it is believed they can see extra colors or patterns in the world around them that humans cannot. These animals often appear to be captivated by and responding to stimulus the rest of us are not seeing.

All faiths and cultures have documentation of these experiences while simultaneously scientists call them fake. Ironically, the Mayo Clinic describes the attack of a migraine patient the exact same way that the spiritual describe devine events, as "hallucinations of colors, patterns, and vibrations." In the Hindu faith, these vibrations or patterns are called auras. In the liturgical art of the Christian faith, they are depicted as halos. After entering a trancelike state, shamans allow what they call "spirit guides of color and pattern" to direct them seeking answers as they visit the underworld.

Because of her degree in social work and years in the public-school system, the mother of twins recognized the boy's autism immediately. Because of that, she had no issues with interactions between her girls and him. It enabled her friendship with the mom to develop without her asking a lot of uncomfortable cautionary questions or listening to defensive answers. She taught her twins about autism and answered their questions softly. She asked them to be his friend, include him, and treat him as special because he was nice, not because he might not be.

When they arrived at the park, each twin took a hand and led the boy to each exhibit. As they talked and giggled to each other, they kept him between them. When one asked him a question, the other would answer for him, and while he was unable to show it, the boy was having a beautiful day.

At one point, one of the twins whispered a secret to her mom. "Hey, Mom, the animals love him!"

"I'm sure they do; he's very sweet, isn't he?"

"No, I mean they love him. Watch how they wake up and come over to him."

"What do you mean, honey?"

"Watch, Mom!"

When they arrived at the next animal enclosure, the

twins stood on either side of him, watching as the boy stood still, save the incessant flapping of his right hand. As soon as the boy stopped at the window, the mandrill came right over. The boy's face was inches from the glass, head to the side, eyes looking back at the creature. Momma Mandrill placed herself in front of him, face inches from the glass. Looking at the creature on the other side of the window, she presented her baby to the boy for approval.

He stopped flapping, and the baby reached out toward him and gently brushed invisible clouds of haze from around the boy's head. Momma Mandrill's eyes followed the space around the baby's hands as if hypnotized by a vortex of color that swirled in the path of the hands. The twins reached up, mimicking the baby, trying to feel what it was seeing. Every person in the packed mandrill viewing area, children included, stood frozen, a witness to this cosmic connection. Slowly other mandrills became hypnotized by the spell, and they drifted over until they stood with the mandrill mom. Their eyes moved in unison with the baby's hands. Finally, one of the more spoiled children in the room interrupted the connection with complaints that it was his turn to play with the baby.

The boy's mom gently guided him away from the window so that this kid could take his turn. But, as soon as the boy moved away, Momma Mandrill mirrored his actions and walked away as well, and the spoiled boy burst into tears.

After a few minutes at another exhibit, everyone was curious to see if what happened was a fluke, so they returned to the mandrill area. They led the boy back to the window, and almost instantly, the momma mandrill and her crowd of mandrills came back to study him.

He put his hand on the window. Separated only by a thin piece of glass, the baby mandrill put his hand on the boy's as the girls giggled and squealed. He lifted his other side to the glass and the little creature matched him. Each time the boy moved his hand, the baby followed him; soon a gentle dance of softly sliding hands merged the auras of the purest souls. The beauty of their movements made oohs and aahs spill in rivers from human lips, while soft moans and purring sounds flowed from bright-blue muzzles on the other side.

The other kids became upset again. They wanted their turn to play with baby mandrill and pushed their way in front of the boy. Again, the boy's mom politely moved him away from the window as the other kids pushed and shoved their way to the glass, and the mandrills retreated. As the boy's group drifted toward another exhibit, an angry man confronted a park employee, yelling, "That boy was hogging all the chances with the baby mandrill." As they walked away, the man was heard insisting that the baby must be brought back to the window for his kid to play with.

BRUSHBACK

The act of toying with or tormenting something before destroying it is known as a game of cat and mouse. Cats are incredibly mean and patient creatures, and if you have never witnessed an actual cat play the game with a real mouse ... well, it is not for the faint of heart.

You would be stunned if you had to watch the amount of torture a cat will inflict upon a poor mouse before allowing it to die. First, the cat disables the mouse and then repeatedly allows it to briefly escape before capturing it. With each capture, it will inflict a little more damage on the pathetic creature, slowly biting and chewing on it just hard enough to inflict more pain, but not enough to put the poor thing out of its misery. Now and then, the cat will set the pitiful creature to the side and sit there patiently watching it suffer before starting another application of torture.

After a day at the zoo, on this particular night at the ballpark, a pitcher and batter played a version of cat and mouse that, during that one at bat, was as brutal as any real cat-and-mouse game could ever be. It was a far more vicious at bat than any baseball historian could remember.

Pitchers and hitters often play games of cat and mouse. When they do, it is essentially a turf war over the inside portion of the plate and the area between it and the batter. Hitters know that they can gain a considerable advantage by crowding, or getting closer to, the plate because it allows them to reach outside pitches, and they get better leverage when they swing at inside ones.

Pitchers also understand the advantages batters gain by

standing close to the plate, so they have a strategy for moving them away from it. This is an approach based on the reality that no hitter wants to feel the sting of a 90 mph fastball. Good Major League pitchers will aim for the extreme outside portions of the plate, but for any pitcher to thrive in the major leagues, they must be able to pitch inside. Great pitchers have the skill to send a message by throwing as close to the batter as they possibly can without actually hitting them, and the message they send is "get away from my plate." This is called a "brushback pitch."

There are degrees of severity concerning the art of the brushback pitch and how it is applied. The politest option is to throw the ball in the area of the batter's waist because they can easily avoid it. At the opposite end of the spectrum, the most impolite option is the high inside fastball aimed just under the chin, as that location will terrify even the most seasoned batter.

Sometimes the threat of a brushback pitch turns into the reality of a batter getting hit by a pitched ball. The baseball term for striking a batsman with a pitched ball is to "bean" them. Most of the time, when pitchers bean someone, it is an accident, and everyone understands this is part of the game, so it is no big deal. There are times, however, when a pitcher hits a batter intentionally, and when they do, it can turn into a huge deal very quickly and trigger a beanball war or even an all-out brawl between entire teams. Most of the biggest fights in baseball history have started over what was thought to be an intentional beaning.

The tricky part is knowing the intent of the pitcher. There are several ways to tell that a beaning is accidental, but you can safely assume that any ball that strikes the arms, legs, or head, or that grazes a batter was an accident. Major League pitchers can throw the ball exactly where they want to, so they aim for the center mass of the butt if they intend to hit a batter. The pitcher's goal is to apply some pain but not injure the hitter, a baseball version of a spanking, and thus, they aim for the butt.

Pitch type is also revealing of intent. Brushback pitches and intentional beanballs are always fastballs because it's too easy to miss with a curve, slider, or knuckler, and quite honestly, they are not all that scary to a Major League hitter. Off-speed pitches are simple to avoid, meaning that unless it's a fastball, there's probably no intent when a batter gets hit.

There is also usually a readily apparent strategic or historical reason to hit a batter. Most often, it is a biblical, eye-for-an-eye retaliation for an earlier brushback, hit batter, or home run. If a player hits a home run and the very next batter gets hit t then that pitch, was retaliation. Retaliation is generally swift, and though it doesn't seem fair, or logical, revenge is inflicted upon the next guy in the lineup, rather than the one who did the deed that angered the pitcher.

However, sometimes brushbacks and beanballs are a tool used by a pitcher for revenge over the smallest possible slight, real or imagined. It might be that a pitcher didn't like that a batter ran too slow or too fast, smiled, talked too loudly, or even just looked toward the wrong place in the wives' section of the stands. Pitchers perceive all these examples as a batter's lack of respect. Next time you see a home run, notice that the hitter probably jogs quickly and keeps his head down. These actions are a sign of respect for the pitcher. In contrast, batters that stand still and watch the flight of the ball, celebrate excessively, taunt, or even move slowly are, according to the unwritten rules of baseball, instigating retaliation.

Then there are madmen. There are not a lot of these evil cats out there, which is good, because these animals are mean creatures and enjoy watching their prey in pain, both physical and mental. The boy's dad was about to bat against one of these types, a man who had made a name for himself as one of the hardest throwing pitchers in baseball and for terrifying batters with high, inside pitches, and most importantly for leading the league in batters hit every year.

This brute liked to hit people with baseballs, and the harder, the better. That king-of-the-jungle reputation com-

ROB MURPHY

bined with the height of the pitching mound made this giant of a man look godlike, and since the boy's dad was only 5'9 ", he was very intimidated. Standing at least 6'6", looking very much like a badass biker dude with his unshaven face, bushy mane, and gnarly tattoos, this Goliath of a man could easily crush the dad if he wanted to.

The boy's dad had only batted a few times in his life, so he only had a superficial knowledge of the intimacy of the cat-and-mouse game pitchers and hitters played concerning crowding the plate. Before getting into the batter's box, the dad wiped the sweat from his strange bulging eyes and looked out at the pitcher before tapping his bat on the toe of his orange shoes, as if he had all the confidence in the world. The reality was that he was terrified and already soaked with sweat. He stood at the inside part of the batter's box simply because he didn't know any better—it was where other hitters seemed to position themselves, so he did too.

He looked out at the pitcher just as the man went into his windup. A 90 mph fastball reaches home plate in 0.417 of a second, and a batter needs to recognize the pitch and start to respond in half that time. The dad didn't have catlike reflexes, so when a fastball came at his chin, instinct took over and he spun out of the way. His teammates yelled in protest from the dugout while the pitchers face squeezed out an evil smirk. The pitcher studied the dusty remains of his victim and how he had screwed himself into the ground, and he laughed at the site of this misfit, sprawled face down in the dirt.

The dad lay there terrified and realized he might have wet his pants, so he gave himself the luxury of a few seconds to think about it before rolling over and sitting up. He then dusted himself off, very much wounded, and got back into the batter's box.

His hands were visibly trembling, and this time he stayed as far away from home plate as he could while still remaining in the batter's box. When the next pitch came in, it was just a powder-puff fastball right over the center of the plate, but that didn't matter. His instinct to survive was in control now, and he had not yet calmed down from the last pitch; thus, his reaction to the second pitch was the stuff of legends. He responded like a bomb had exploded in front of him. He jumped spastically out of the batter's box and then involuntarily drilled himself into the dirt once again. Even his teammates chuckled at this pathetic display of cowardice.

The pitcher was one happy cat and made no effort to hide his glee at the torture he was inflicting on this insignificant little creature. He had made up his mind that he was going to slowly chew on this mouse of a man as long as possible before finishing him off.

Eventually, the boy's dad got back up, dusted off, and some unknown higher power moved him slowly back to the batter's box. He tried to gain control over how terrified he was long enough to continue batting against this menace. Again, he looked out and made eye contact with the beast, who sneered that wicked grin one more time just as he went into his windup.

The ball flew in with an evil hiss, another high, inside fastball right at his head. This pitch could not have missed by more than a couple of hairs. Once more he threw himself into the safety of the ground, and if there was any doubt last time, now the father was sure he had wet his pants.

As he lay there covered in dirt, sweat, and urine, feeling like something the cat chewed up, he heard the umpire issue a warning to the pitcher. From his seat in the red dirt of home plate, he looked out at the pitcher, prowling the mound, purring with satisfaction, in admiration of his efforts.

The whole world was laughing at the fraud unmasked, and the dad's mind raced at the thought of this public execution. Head down, eyes shut, waiting for the executioner's blade, he remembered the process that brought him here and all the self-doubt he had back then. Of how he never wanted to do this, and most of all, how badly he did not want to be here right now.

David had actual skills and the power of youth when he took on Goliath. David also wanted the fight. In contrast, the boy's dad did not have the youth, skill, or the will to fight, and was instead embarrassed, miserable, and terrified. His batting was a stunt, a whim that was now horribly out of control. He had only done this for his family and the money. Now he was utterly humiliated, overmatched, and undeserving of the opportunity to be playing in the presence of gods. He dropped his head, shut his eyes, and he gave up.

After a few seconds, he opened them again, and his gaze shifted to the stands for the first time. He saw the chaos of frenzied sinners cheering as he was about to be fed to a lion. He stood up, intending to quit, and began the long, slow walk back to his dugout while the crowd continued its thirst for blood. Then he saw his son standing perfectly still among the waves of anarchy rolling past him.

At that exact moment, the batboy ran up to him, offering a towel to clean the dirt off his glasses. The dad realized that he could hardly see, so he took off the glasses and buried his face in the towel to wipe away some of the mud. He then whispered thanks to the batboy, and as he began to clean his lenses, he thought about what he should do.

The biblical underdog won because he had planned for an unconventional fight—he did the unexpected. "What's my plan . . . what's he thinking, what does he expect?" he whispered to himself.

He put on his glasses, smiled at the batboy, tossed him the towel, and looked up at his son one more time. Their eyes met for one long moment, and suddenly, it was clear to him what he needed to do.

He started with a slow, deliberate walk, almost strutting, back to the batter's box. He took the time to circle all the way around behind the umpire and looked around the ballpark, as if he were out for a stroll on a sunny day, before turning back toward the batter's box.

He then did something nobody was expecting, stopping just outside the batter's box. Now proudly wearing the dirt, sweat, and pee, he took four very dramatic, deep bows, like a theatrical Shakespearean actor, to all corners of the stadium.

With each bend, the crowd's noise grew until it reached a crescendo as he rose from the final bow. With the attention of each sinner on his every move, he let loose a massive, exaggerated spit wad toward the pitcher, a clear, disgusting signal in his opening salvo to say that this mouse had some fight left in him.

The dad moved back in the box, looking out at the pitcher with his back hand extended flat and open to the umpire—the universal sign that batters use to maintain timeout while they dig in and get ready. The umpire waited as he put both hands on the bat.

"Ready, buddy?" the ump said in a low voice.

The dad gave a little nod with his head, still focused on the pitcher, and in a voice loud enough to be heard by the pitcher said, "c'mon, you piece of crap, throw the ball."

The umpire signaled the pitcher, who started his windup. Instantly the dad raised his hand and yelled, "Time," and stepped out of the batter's box. The umpire immediately stopped the play, but it was too late to stop, and the pitcher continued his throw to the plate, a perfect strike, lost to a more perfectly timed timeout. The beast growled an angry "aww, c'mon" to nobody in particular as he spun away from the plate in anger.

Everyone in the stadium could sense the change in the tone of the at bat. The dad looked around the stadium as if bored with the whole experience, taking his time, pretending to prepare before getting back in the batter's box again, hand held out at the umpire. He looked out at the pitcher, spat, and one more time the umpire started the play. One more time, just as the pitcher began his windup, the dad called time and stepped out of the box while the pitch continued on its way.

The pitcher exploded in a fury of spittle-laden obscenities and violent gestures toward home plate. The stadium roared as everybody could see that the giant's once jovial mood had turned to rage. Pitchers hate it when hitters call time like this because it takes a great deal of effort to stop a throw midway through; it throws off their rhythm and otherwise wastes a perfectly good pitch.

The dad knew he could not compete with the over-whelming power of this man, so he planned to make a show of this final Major League at bat, and to provoke the monster into being stupid. Strategically, he wanted to make this cat so mad that he would throw another brushback pitch. If he could do that, it would make the count three balls and two strikes, and the pitcher would have to throw another strike. Then he might have a chance. Almost every sinner in the stadium sensed what the next pitch would be.

Once more, he moved back into the batter's box, looking at the pitcher. But, this time, he crowded the plate, position-ing himself as close to it as the rules would allow, with his toes right on the chalk line. He made sure to leave his hands out over the plate. He then nodded to the umpire, and the crazed pitcher went into a furious windup, releasing a ball that made an evil buzz as it traveled at the dad's head. This time, rather than freak out and wet his pants, he stood stoic, perfectly still, calmly moving only his head the smallest possible amount required to allow the whistling ball to travel past. Rather than cheers and protests, a low "ooh" moved through the crowd, as the blood-thirsty sinners in it realized that this mouse no longer feared that cat.

It was now a three ball, two strike count with the bases loaded, and the next pitch had to be a strike. The plan worked perfectly, the beast was furious, clawing at the dirt, his mind lost in the chaos of battle but confined by the rules of base-ball. The manager called a timeout to calm his man. Once at the mound, he tried to rein him in, distract him. The manager needed to soothe the beast, to keep his gaze away from his tor-mentor, who stood calmly, waiting and ready at home plate. The dad never left the batter's box, and instead looked directly at the beast, mocking him, motionless, bat on his shoulder, as if impatient with the delay.

The dad had succeeded in destroying the pitcher's self-control, and all that was left was the kill. Finally, the umpire broke up the meeting and the giant glared at him once more. The dad knew this pitch was going to be a fastball over the plate because the pitcher had no other options; all the dad needed to do was figure out which type of fastball he would throw.

When a pitcher throws a two-seam fastball, the laces are very visible as the ball rotates bottom to top, and the laces form what looks like parallel vertical red lines as the ball spins through the air—like train tracks coming at you. A two-seam fastball is harder to throw, but most important to the dad was that he knew that a two-seam fastball moves toward the right as it flies through the air. When the pitcher throws a four-seam fastball, the stitches tumble end over end at such a fast speed that the seams disappear into a muddy blur. A four-seam fastball is a much easier pitch to throw, and the ball stays perfectly straight as it moves through the air. The big cat had just thrown him a four-seam fastball.

After he hit the ball, he raised his arms in the touchdown formation, bat held in one hand as high in the air as possible, and he stood there watching the ball for the entirety of its flight. When it finally disappeared over the center-field fence, he was still holding his bat high above his head, waiting to make sure the pitcher saw him.

Only then did he start his long slow jog around the bases, gaze fixed on the pitcher all the while. By the time he rounded third base, he had slowed to the most leisurely pace possible, and it was all the pitcher could do to contain himself. With about fifteen feet to go, the boy's dad started to walk, looking at the pitcher, smiling and laughing at him, and pumped his fist the rest of the way.

It is quite possible that no batter has ever shown up, or disrespected a pitcher this badly. At the exact moment that he triumphantly jumped with both feet on home plate, the pitcher tackled him, driving him into the ground. At least ten of the dad's teammates had gathered to greet him. They jumped to his defense, and a massive pile of writhing bodies quickly formed in the area around home plate. The infielders soon piled on, followed by the outfielders, dugouts, and bullpens. In the chaos, somehow, the dad squirted out the back of the pile and disappeared into the clubhouse.

VIBRATIONS

T he Detroit River is one of the world's busiest waterways and forms a border between the United States and Canada. Its deepest point is only fifty-four feet, but at an average speed of 7 mph, a large volume of water passes through it, and it all ultimately spills over Niagara Falls. In the 1920s, during Prohibition, a great deal of alcohol also passed through the Detroit river. While Prohibition was called "the Noble Experiment," it actually resulted in the most significant increase in crime in American history and led directly to organized crime in this country.

Most of the members of Detroit's Purple Gang, at least early on, came from just one small neighborhood: the Paradise Valley neighborhood on Hastings Street in Detroit's lower east side. When those men were kids, almost all of them went to a single small school called the Bishop School. There is no apparent reason that such a vast reign of crime could emerge from a tiny area, but there are several theories for how they came to be named the Purple Gang. The most fun theory is that the people of the neighborhood gave them that title after the color of bad meat, "because they, too, were rotten!"

In the Detroit of the 1920 and 30s, the Purple Gang were kings of the Detroit gangs. This gang was feared for its casual application of extreme violence, and it had a resume that included murder, executions, kidnapping, gambling, and the real money-maker—bootlegging.

Most of the bootlegging involved bringing alcohol across the Detroit River from Canada. The small islands in the river that could be used as hiding places made it almost impossible for police to stop the bootleggers. The best island for this purpose was Belle Isle because it was wide, thin, and very close to the American coast. This allowed the gang to remain hidden for all but the shortest portion of the trip. The Purple Gang became so successful that Al Capone didn't try to fight them but instead partnered with them to supply alcohol for his operations in Chicago at the height of Prohibition.

Today was a day off for the old man who mowed the lawns at the ballpark, and the boy sat in the boat between his dad and the old man. The trio was fishing today directly in the path of where the Purple Gang made its many runs across the Detroit River. They were just a few hundred feet off the southern tip of Belle Isle and a hundred yards or so closer to Canada than the United States. Back in the 1920s, the Purple Gang would leave Canada with a load of goods hidden from American law enforcement by Belle Isle. Several hidden spotters on the American side would signal them when the coast was clear. Then, the bootleggers had just a short trip from the Canadian side of the Isle to the American shore, where they could disappear into the streets of Detroit.

The dad and boy had fished together a lot on some of the inland lakes of Michigan, but never in a big river. It seemed essential to the old man that they learn how to do it the correct way. At least a couple of times a week, the trio would go out in the river in the old man's small motorboat to spend some time fishing. While the old man was reticent at work, he talked a mile a minute to the boy once they were out in the boat. Today he was trying to teach the finer points of a fishing technique called "vertical jigging."

Trolling is when you drop a fishing lure or jig in the water behind a boat and then move the boat through the water at a slow speed. The jig or bait is designed to wiggle or dance in the water and mimic the actions of a small fish, with the hope of getting a larger fish to bite it.

In contrast, vertical jigging is when you drop anchor and

fish from the same spot without moving. The action of vertical jigging is simply to drop the jig all the way to the bottom of the river and then reel it back up. In a fast-moving river like the Detroit River, you gain both the horizontal action of the river pushing on the lure and the vertical movement of it being reeled to the surface. This dual action turns out to be an excellent way to fish, at least in the Detroit River.

The old man was trying to impress upon the boy the value of reeling the jig up at different speeds, sometimes very slow, sometimes fast, and sometimes changing the pace. The idea is that different types of fish hang out at different levels of the water table and respond to varying types of action as the bait moves through the water. The only way to figure out what they like is to mix it up each time.

It was clear that the boy was flourishing with all this new stimulus. On the river, the boy had an unlimited supply of flickering, glittering, and shimmers from all sides. He also had the tactile sensation of water at his fingertips and the uninterrupted attention of two adults. As the old man spoke, the boy as was his way, did not make eye contact, but he was nonetheless very attentive. The boy would hold perfectly still with his head tilted slightly back and turned sideways, as if looking away from the man. He would then turn his eyes to look back at the old man, staring intensely just to the side of his face. He was clearly concentrating hard to understand what he was being told. The dad had always been curious, and he wanted desperately to understand what the boy thought and saw when he did this with his head.

When the old man stopped talking, the boy would hold the pose for five or six long seconds. Then he would suddenly move to try and do what he had just been told. Most of the time, he did quite well, and it was clear the old man very much enjoyed the teaching aspect of this relationship. Not all teaching in the boy's life went as well. So far, going to school had been a disappointment, but more for the parents than the boy. Kids were not always kind to the boy, and while the majority treated him well, there were still bullies who would do him wrong. Sometimes it was just verbal teasing, and other times it got physical. When that happened, the school did little to stop it. Some days the boy would arrive home with bruises and welts, but because he was mute, the parents would never know the story behind them.

While it bothered the parents, the boy didn't notice the kids that picked on him. They were just dull, droning gray shadows in a world full of shifting colors and patterns that moved around the people and things he encountered. His was an entire world of vistas blooming with rhythm and vibration, while bullies were flat and dull, lacking the dimensions of depth and texture that he preferred. When bullies appeared to him, they emerged from billows of gray clouds that seemed to squeeze out from their faces. The bullies that picked on him were lifeless crispies, with skins of small sharp shards that chewed at each other across the surface. Only when bullies physically hurt him was he really aware of them, and only because the hurt they inflicted caused ripples in the vibrations he preferred to watch. Physical pain didn't hurt the boy, but it caused colors to separate and fall into thick clouds of dark shadows that erupted like a cyclone. These would spew green sparks that would fly at him, blind him, and hide the preferred vibrations from him.

Given all the other stimuli, the bullies the boy encountered were not just easy to ignore, they were hard to notice. His was a world of kaleidoscopic sensations that grew and shifted and morphed steadily. Like a plucked guitar string, his normality was full of colors, patterns, and sounds. Sounds that echoed, bent backward, then repeated, they stretched and ripped apart, then re-assembled and turned into scratches that flew away. Then they swooped and disappeared into other shapes and smells and emerged at him from the other side of things.

His was a world of portals through which he could only glimpse the three-dimensional reality the rest of us exist in. His existence had many more dimensions, and each of those had levels, tangents, parallels, subdivisions, and perpendiculars that scraped at him. They became translucent films that bubbled, and fluids that dissolved, froze, and then crumbled into shards that spun and flipped off into the distance before wrapping around him again.

The boy was happy in his world, even if happiness was not an emotion he could express in a way that others would understand. Still, it was one he felt always. People were the most fascinating part of his world. For reasons he did not understand, they tried to interact with him, and each other, while inanimate things did not. Every person had a shape surrounded by a color and a pattern. These would spin, morph, and move, and as the people adjusted their gazes to or from him those designs would change and shift within the plasma.

When he looked at a crowd of people, he saw the shapes of hundreds of colors writhing together and bouncing off one another, and it calmed him. While in a crowd of people, one of them would inevitably glance at him. When that happened, their face would emerge from the mass and grow large. This would last for a second, then the face would pull back into the writhing collective, and another would step forward in a process that would endlessly repeat, but only for a second or two each time.

When a friend would come to him, the effect was magnified. As a rule, the people that were nice to him, or even each other, had warm colors, and those colors became brighter as they interacted with him, or he grew to know them. The patterns of these people were soft and moved slowly. The surface of their skin glowed with beautifully intricate patterns or waves of lines that moved concentrically over the surface of the skin like fingerprints but flowed like ripples in endless rivers of warmth.

In the boy's world, most things had a color and a pattern, although not all things had vibrations. Rocks, for example, were just rocks, and to the boy looked the same they did to everyone else. Things like a grass lawn or vegetation generally moved, but very slowly and only as the light changed or people walked upon them. A short grass field moved very, very slowly, while a meadow with tall grasses changed much more fluidly as wind and light shifted. It was a matter of fact to him that everything affects everything else, is part of, came from, and will one day be everything else.

Trees and the way light moved through them were the boy's favorite things to interact with. He could study each individual leaf as it fluttered like a diamond in the light. He would come to know the characteristics and dimensions of every single leaf, and watched how it changed and grew over summer and when it fell to earth in the fall and how its color would slowly climb back into the ground before the snows came.

Like trees, the surface of the water was equally hypnotic to him. Both could calm the rest of the world for him, at least momentarily, and allow him to try to see into the world that the rest of us see. He very much wanted to do this.

The boy didn't have a way to describe this but the rest of the world might think of them as holes. At times when he could calm the chaos, those holes would flow by him, offering glimpses of our world, and that fascinated him. He would see faces squeeze into view, and mouths move, and see words spilling from those mouths that then flew away. Sometimes the voices spoke slowly and were very clear, as if very important things, essential things even more important things, were out there for him to learn. He sensed he should listen to those faces and try to understand those secrets, that they might be vital, so he should work hard to understand them. Most of the time, holes would collapse, and the colors would come again talking at him in hisses, scraps, and clicks before he could understand the message.

But on some days like this, when water flickered or trees glittered, the holes slowed down and opened wide, and he could get a good long look by stepping through to the other side. He could come into this dull world of just three dimensions with faces that slowly swallow air, and take a few awkward first steps. He could reach out a toe, trying to feel where the toe ended and the surface started, before stepping out of his alien craft and twisting that toe on this surface so new to him. Today on the river was a great day because he got to go out into the world on the other side of the hole for a long time, and it was so calm and still, and pleasant for him to experience.

The peace of it all overwhelmed him. As the old man talked, his head was surrounded by soft yellow undulation that mesmerized the boy, and that he wanted to go on forever. He could hear the words clearly and understand the meaning and was excited to try vertical jigging of all things.

The dad had grown up in the world of merely dropping the hook in the water, the don't-mess-with-it-until-something-bites-it approach to fishing. So, it was fun for him to see someone so passionate about the different ways to reel up a line. The dad loved how the old man would get so excited when he thought the boy did it just right, and how the boy was clearly responding to this interaction.

The lure that they used was called a "silver spinner," which is a very simple, easy-to-use lure. Besides the hook, it features a single silver, feather-shaped piece of metal designed to spin around the hook as it moves through the water. Each time the boy would pull his line, he would spend several minutes watching it flutter through the current at the side of the boat before dropping it down again. Sometimes the boy would stop and watch the light as it flickered off the water. He did this for long periods of time, and the old man seemed to understand that these times were essential to the boy.

Walleye and lake whitefish were the fish the old man sought. Every time they went, the group did well. Most of the fish were released back into the river, but usually the old man would keep one for dinner. Given where they lived, it didn't seem right to the dad to be cutting up fresh fish in the kitchen, so they always let the fish they caught go.

Over time, the old groundskeeper and the boy had become fast friends. In contrast to everybody else at the ballpark, the old man had a lot of time to do nothing. His primary job was taking care of the field. After that, he was there just in case there was some field emergency, and that never happened, so he was always around. He was content with his lot in life, perfectly happy doing exactly what he was doing, not caught trying to move up the corporate ladder. Like the boy, he wasn't much of a talker, so the two paired well together, and most importantly, they enjoyed the company of one another.

However, one day, the dad saw the old man approaching with a concerned look on his face. He was doing his best to run toward the dad as he did his stretching in right field. The poor man was near tears as he told the dad, "I think there's something wrong. I'm not sure, but he's not moving much. He's in the tunnel."

The trailer was parked in its slot under the stands in the maintenance tunnel just inside the right-field corner. It has been backed into its space so that the back end was about eighteen inches from the wall. As soon as the dad saw the boy, he knew instantly he was fine and moved quickly to soothe the frantic old man.

When the dad found him, the boy was lying in the dirt on his stomach. He was in the back of a dirt cart that was used when the pitching mound needed maintenance. It was an extended flat trailer kept full of dirt for when new soil is required. The boy allowed his neck to rest on the tailgate so that his head spilled over the edge. This enabled him to look straight down at the ground, where he had found something of interest. His dad peered over the edge to see what it was, then sat down next to the boy to look.

On the ground below the boy was a long thin trail of ants making its way along the concrete floor right next to where it met the wall. Within the train were seven or eight clumps of ants. Each clump was a little different in size and shape, but each was a mass of ants straining together to move bits of what looked like a broken cookie back to a crack in the floor several feet away.

The dad remembered that the boy liked to watch ants in the yard, but it occurred to him that the boy had never had a clear view of what they were doing. At home, the ants would emerge from and disappear into blades of grass, and here the boy had an uninterrupted view of the entire process.

It took a clump of ants a very long time to move its prize from a point in front of them to several feet away to the hole in the ground. It wasn't the same ants that moved the thing the entire way, but if you watched closely, you could see the prize being passed along within the train as new ants were added to the clump and old ones fell behind. Some of the bits of cookie were too big to go down the hole. When that happened, the mass of ants around the thing would increase many times greater until somehow the cookie in the center of the celebration would break apart and then be carried down the hole.

The dad leaned in close to the boys' head and spoke softly in his ear. "Those are ants. They live in tunnels that they make beneath floors, a tunnel just like the one we are in right now only smaller. They work very hard all day looking for food to bring home. See those big clumps of ants? Right in the middle of them is some piece of food that they found. It looks like they have a piece of cookie, and they are working to carry that food down into their home. Right now, the babies are in their homes are under this floor, waiting with their moms for this food. See how they travel in lines like that? They do that, so none of them get lost. The door to their home is over there, where they all go into the floor.

The boy turned over quickly and rose to a sitting position, causing the old man to take a few steps away. The boy sat like this for a minute or two. Then, he turned back over, looked back down at the ants, was once again perfectly still.

While the boy had seen ants before, they did not look, move, or sound like anything else. Even when they were not moving, the surface of the ant was many layers deep. And each layer vibrated differently, making them seem both translucent and solid at the same time. Ants did not have colors surrounding them like other beings but they did have colors. But the color from ants was different, it glowed and escaped at the elbows, knees, and neck while the surfaces were dull and colorless like charcoal. All the life he saw in them was only in the eyes. They had large eyes that glowed a single solid color, and each group of ants burned a different color. The ones returning with food glowed warm, and the ones leaving home glowed cold. Mixed among them were a few ants whose eyes moved quickly from blue to green and sometimes turned bright red.

But it was the sounds that ants made that the boy found so surprising. Each ant made hundreds of distinct sounds all at the same time. They constantly sang to all the other ants, all at the same time. It was a sonic blender all looping together, yet each noise was easily identifiable and understood within the blend. The way that ants communicated made so much more sense to the boy than the method that humans used.

Then, suddenly, the boy jumped up and walked over to the old man. He took his hand, and the two friends walked out of the tunnel and out onto the field.

3:16

One of the greatest plays of all time happened in 1981 during game two of the ALCS, when left fielder Dave Winfield jumped high over the left-field wall and took a home run away from Oakland's Tony Armas. If you watch the video and look closely, you will notice the fans seated in that area dove out of the way. Whether they did this out of self-preservation, or to maximize Mr. Winfield's chance of catching the ball, will never be known.

When this incident happened baseballs version of the bible was called the Official Baseball Rule Book. In that book there is a rule titled 6.01 (e) (3.16). In the sport it is known colloquially as 3.16, and like its similar sounding biblical counterpart it is one of this book best known rules. It states:

"No interference shall be allowed when a fielder reaches over a fence, railing, rope, or into a stand to catch a ball. He does so at his own risk. However, should a spectator reach out on the playing field side of such fence, railing or rope, and plainly prevent the fielder from catching the ball, then the batsman should be called out for spectator's interference."

The television network covering the event had six different cameras at the game. None of them showed a definitive replay angle, but that doesn't matter because this play happened long ago, in the days before video replays were used to confirm or change a call. On that day, without the benefit of replay, the umpire signaled that it was a home run.

At the dads forth major league at bat, something similar occurred to what happened to that 1981 game. The details of the play are very simple. The left fielder ran at the wall, kicked off it to gain height, and made a spectacular leap, reaching far above the fence to catch the ball, just like Dave Winfield did back in 1981.

That the player had his glove in position to catch the ball was very clear. It was also clear that the ten-year-old girl, sitting with her Girl Scout troop in the front row, turned her head, shut her eyes, stuck out her five-dollar glove, and stole the ball from the million-dollar-a-year outfielder. After she caught it, the girl was jumping up and down excitedly as were her fellow scouts.

That is, until the big, hairy, mean-looking left fielder started climbing the wall, screaming and spitting at her in a furious, red-faced tirade. Terrified, the entire Girl Scout troop started crying and left the stadium. The fans in attendance sided with the Girls Scouts and the audience booed and threw things at the outfielder until they took him out of the game.

It was "plainly clear" that she reached for the ball, but given her eyes were shut and the head was turned, it's hard to argue malice on her part. Beyond that, it was not at all clear that she reached out over the field, or even what side of the fence the catch happened on. The best replay angle showed that the girl reached sideways to catch the ball. She did not lean over the field, or even make an aggressive effort for the ball; she just stuck her glove out and accidentally caught it.

Once the ball crosses over the top of the wall, the fan has every right to catch it. If, on the other hand, the fan reaches just one thin mint over the wall, it is fan interference, and the batter is out. In this case, it just was not clear, so the dad of the boy had just hit his forth home run in a row, breaking a Major League record for most consecutive home runs to start a career.

It is a play that has been talked about in San Francisco forever because that hit turned out to be a go-ahead home run, ultimately the game winner, and that loss caused San Francisco to fall out of first place. People plead their case that the call was wrong or right for years, but either way, it was clear that the ball was over the wall. On a side note, that Girl Scout sold more cookies during the next week than any other Girl Scout in the history of scouting.

GRILLED CHEESE?

And so, it ended. The family was told all along that it would not last, and they could expect this experience to end. It had been a wonderful time in their lives, but all things end. This was moving day, out of the art deco palace and on to something more in the realm of mere mortals.

It had been four weeks since the ten-thousand-square-foot palace became their home. The short-term luxury became a month-long fantasy, thanks to the dad's accidental success. Now, the team needed the palace back for the corporate events it was intended for.

In reality, once the initial amazement wore off, the family lived in one or two of the smaller rooms, just like at home. This palace was like a fancy tuxedo you rent for a wedding: you know you are supposed to be impressed with it, but you never feel like you belong in it. Still, at weddings, you get lots of photos while you are all dressed up pretty, so they made sure to take pictures of themselves in every room.

Along with a moving crew, the mother of twins and her girls showed up to help and get the family settled in their new place.

"We got you an apartment just down the street from here, in the same building we live in. It's nice, modern, spotless, and safe too," said the mother of twins.

"Where are your things? Are you packed?" She looked down at the half-dozen or so white trash bags and the framed San Diego Zoo poster placed near the door.

"Yep, that's it, those over there," said the mother of the boy.

"Oh, is that all you have? Where is all your stuff, your luggage?" the twins' mother asked with an amazed look on her face.

"Honey, that's all we have—remember?"

"Remember what?"

"We didn't know we were going to do this. We didn't pack. This is just the stuff we've bought since we've been here."

"Well," she said, looking at the workers, "why don't you guys walk this stuff down the street to the apartment?"

"Excuse me, ma'am, but we were told to bring out the truck. You hired us for the whole day" said the older man.

"Of course, I know, don't worry about that; you're just going to have an easy day, that's all," she said, reassuring the men that they would get their day's pay.

She guessed the oldest man was in his mid to late fifties. Like all of them, he was dressed in comfortable-looking coveralls with the name "Pops" embroidered in quotes ID style on the right side of his chest. His appearance was unremarkable in every other way but he knew how to blend politely within the service industry, just as the three other men did. They were much younger; all appeared to be about the same age, somewhere in their late twenties. All were well groomed, polite, and attentive, and each crewed a hand truck ready to move things on command.

"Well, shall we? To the truck?" commanded the mother of twins, pointing like she imagined a general leading troops might do.

And with that, the three young movers picked up the trash bags and the momma mandrill poster, and they all made their way down to the truck parked in the loading dock.

The truck was a forty-eight-foot semi "Kentucky" moving trailer. Except for the cab being more extended than usual, it was like any other semi rig you might see on a freeway. It certainly did not seem like anything unusual. There were three broad sets of double doors on each side as well as the large double doors at the back that had already been opened.

The movers walked right in, set down the bags, and the boss turned back and said, "That's that! Break time, men!" Then he looked up with a smile.

The group stood at the back of the trailer and looked down the long, brightly lit tunnel. One of the twins leaned her head inside and said, in a very loud voice, "Hello." She listened as the echo sounded back at her. Very quickly, all three kids were making echoes, banging on the walls, and running back and forth inside the trailer. The workers were charmed by this and stood aside to let them play.

After a minute, the Pops moved over to the mother of twins. "This truck is used for long-haul moving. Would you like to let the kids look around, give them a tour of the cabin, honk the horns?"

"I don't know if the kids would like it, but I've always wanted to see the inside of one of these things," said the mom of twins gleefully.

Inside, the cab was gorgeous! The air was fresh and filled with the smell of warm bread and cookies. Everything was bright, shiny, clean, and amazingly well designed, in the mid-century modern style.

The puzzled ladies looked around like they suddenly found themselves in Oz. The room featured multilayered soffit lighting, a ceiling fan, and high-end elegant track lighting. The driver's and passengers' seats were able to rotate and recline within the environment of the living space. There was a beautiful kitchen complete with Pewabic Pottery backsplash, fitted with a full-size fridge, stove, as well as running water.

On either side of the room were two comfortable looking couches, another recliner, and above, lots of cabinets and storage space. Behind and above the driver's seat was a reasonably large TV, and hidden toward the rear was an ornate door that led to a small but very nice, private bathroom.

"Can I offer some coffee, tea, soda, something to eat?" asked the older man. "Grilled cheese, perhaps?"

"Wow! This is beautiful. I should check on the kids—" said the mom of twins.

"Here you go." Pops clicked a remote-control device and four views appeared on TV of what was happening in the back of the truck, as well as on either side of it. She could see the kids were OK and happily playing.

"Grilled cheese sounds just lovely," said the mother of twins as if playing along with the joke.

"Do you have sparkling water?" asked the boys mom joining in with the joke.

"Hang on a minute," Pops interrupted, and he pressed another button on the remote. Immediately both side walls started sliding outward, creating another eight feet of floor space in the center of the room.

"Oh my." said the mom.

"This is amazing! What is—?"

Then Pops pressed another, and a tabletop rose out of the floor. In a well-practiced dance the other men instantly slid chairs into place around the table and signaled the ladies to sit. As they watched this rehearsed ballet the ladies voiced their amazement.

"Shut up!" whispered the mom backing away as if dangerous things were happening.

"Are you kidding me? This is so cool!"

Then he touched a third button, and one of the sliding walls begins to open. A large bay window seat was revealed that spanned the full length of the wall opposite the kitchen, complete with beautiful window treatments.

"This is incredible!" said the mother of twins as if she had just seen a great magic trick.

"No way!"

In a blur, the men shifted into full speed, choreographed, gourmet restaurant mode. Quickly, the third man spread a dark tablecloth, and another set the table, complete with the matching place settings.

Sparkling waters were placed before the women, and a

ring of vegetables followed, while another man set down a selection of dips in the center of the vegetable ring.

Then, in the tradition of seasoned waiters, they took turns introducing each of the dips. The oldest of the young men who had the name "Red" embroidered on his ID badge went first. "I have for you several flavorings as you wait for your food. This is labneh with pistachios, parsley, lemon, and sumac."

Then seamlessly "Sparky" offered, "Over here is a sesame sweet potato miso."

Immediately "Owl" chimed in, "My favorite is this Mayan pumpkin seed dip."

And without hesitation "Red" displayed a bowl and pronounced, "And I think you will like this. It's Artichokes with avocado-anchovy dip."

"And finally, a classic homemade buttermilk ranch." said all three of the young men in unison is if it were a grand finale and they were taking a bow.

"Who are you people?" Said both ladies in an echoed unison response.

"Where did all this come from?" spewed the mother of twins looking around for a hidden restaurant nearby.

"This is incredible." whispered the mom considering the beautiful bounty before her.

"Are we on hidden TV?"

"No, ma'am," said the older man with a smile.

The three workers then went about the business of preparing to cook while the oldest man sat with them.

Hidden shelves flipped up or were pulled out, and various foods appeared. The bread was sliced, and eggs cracked all with lightning speed. The two women are lost, fascinated by the efficiency of what was happening behind them, like they were watching master chefs on a snotty cooking show.

"This is like that TV show" said the mom in stunned whisper.

"What do you call this?" asked the mother of twin, holding her arms out and wiggling her fingers to indicate the room they are in.

"Well, we call it our home," said Pops proudly.

"Home? You men live here?" The mother of twins looked around, stunned at how perfectly clean, bright, and fresh the place was, with not a thing out of place, nor a blemished or worn spot anywhere.

"At least a lot of the time. We travel a lot."

"What's the correct name for this, what are we in?" said the younger woman.

"If you mean this room, the industry calls them sleepers, but we modified it a little." Pops answered proudly.

Stunned yet again the mom interrupted, "Wait, sleeper? Are there beds in here too?"

"Oh yes, ma'am, there's four of them."

"Where?" puzzled, the mother of twins looked around the room in search of beds.

"They're hidden right now, but one is up there. Back behind the bath, that's mine, and these couches turn into beds, very comfortable too."

"This is a bed?

"No that's a couch. Underneath it is the bed. It flips over."

"Really? But there's no privacy?"

"Oh sure there is. The walls close around them—perfectly private, and quiet too!"

"We like it," interjected Owl, "It's nice."

"I am stunned! I had no idea this was possible," said the mom.

"It all looks brand new how long have you done this?" continued the mother of twins.

"I've been at this my whole life, my two sons—" Two of the men, Red and Sparky, respectfully nodded, smiled and simultaneously said, "Ma'am."

"They have kind of joined me over the years. We've had this rig about ten years?" said Pops, looking at one of the men for confirmation.

"And over there, my sister's boy."

"Ma'am" said Owl.

"Yep, that's right, ten years in September," he responded.

"Do most movers cook grilled cheese for the people they move?" asked the mom.

"I don't think so. We like to eat well, live well, so we cook. We take grilled cheese pretty serious."

With that, each of the young men introduced sandwiches and once again Red went first. "This is a pear, bacon, and brie grilled cheese on homemade sourdough. It comes with maple-bacon potato salad and fried kale."

Sparky instantly placed another sandwich in front of the woman. "I give you our garlic confit and baby arugula grilled cheese. It is quite wonderful, and it comes with caramelized baked beans and fried mustard greens. The bread is a ciabatta. That is a kind of Italian white bread; it's pretty great."

"Did you guys make the bread too?" asked the Mom in genuine amazement.

"Of course," said Pops with a mischievous smile.

"Pop makes the bread," offered Red proudly.

Then Owl stepped forward with a platter, displayed it and said, "And this is Monterey chicken grilled cheese with basted chicken, bacon, barbecue sauce, and cheese on our Irish soda bread. And with it, we have mustard potato salad and fried spinach. We love fried greens."

Sparky immediately jumped back to present another platter: "And last we have artichoke-arugula pesto grilled cheese on pumpernickel."

"We bought that bread," said Red as he and the other young men looked away as if embarrassed by the thought of serving store bought bread.

"Sorry," said Pops sheepishly.

"No greens this time?" said the mother of twins sarcastically trying to rescue Pops from the scorn of the others.

Instantly Sparky placed another plate on the table and it is heaped with fried green tomatoes.

"This is—stunning—" said the mom in disbelief.

"Is that all?" said the mother of twins sarcastically. "What's he making over there?

"These are American on Wonder Bread for the kids," said Red at the stove. "We have fries for them, but they can they have some apple slices with caramel dip if you like, or a juice box?"

The two ladies were dumbfounded and broke into a spontaneous standing ovation. Offering all sorts of verbal praise, the mother of twins ended with: "Can we hire you to move again tomorrow?"

"Please, sit?" said Pops and with that polite request they all sat down. "We don't have guests usually, but we like to cut up all the sandwiches, so we can share, mix and match, sample. Would that be OK?"

"Yes, yes, yes," said the mother of twins clapping excitedly as the kids entered. "Oh, here they come!"

"Momma, this is so pretty. Is this a playhouse?" Said one twin looking around.

"Can we have some?" offered the other.

Red led the kids to their table and said, "We got some for you too. Would you sit down right here, and we'll get you set up." The kids sat on the window seat and a hidden table is pulled out of the wall and quickly food was placed for them.

"Dig in, kids," said Red before returning to his seat.

"Momma, I love grilled cheese!"

"This is a great restaurant, Momma, thank you."

As they ate, they talked.

"This food is fantastic; how did this happen," said the mother twins with a mouth full of food.

Pops looked around the room at the boys and pretending to not understand the questions real meaning said, "Well, we cooked it."

"No, I mean I didn't expect to find a five-star restaurant in front of a semitruck; this blows my mind," said the mother of twins.

"Now, how long have you done this? Oh my God, try this; it's incredible." The mom held her fork out to her friends' mouth.

"Well, I've been in the moving game for about thirty years now, and my boys here have just joined over the years."

"No, I mean the cooking."

"This is marvelous," groaned the mom.

"Well, we need to eat."

"This might be the coolest thing I've ever seen. You should go into business," insisted the mother of twins.

"This is our business," said Pops insisting right back!

"Do that one, try that," moaned the mom as she pointed to the beans.

"No, I mean the cooking part." She tried the baked beans and made a face of total bliss.

"Is there catsup for my fries, Momma?" asked a twin.

"No, too many rules," said Pop, "we just like a good meal," before reaching over and setting catsup down in front of the child. "Is she OK with—?"

"She's fine." The mother of twins waved her hand and nodded. "I'm sorry, but I gotta ask: have you moved for us before?"

"Well, ma'am, yes, we've moved a lot of families for your company."

"Can I have more juice?" asked the other twin?

"I got it," said Owl who happened to be closest to the fridge.

"I'm sorry, I don't remember you guys. How many times, how long ago?"

"Oh, these greens are . . . here taste that," said, the mom holding out a fork full of food for her friend to sample.

Pop considered the question a bit then responded, "Last week was the last time. Three or four times this year, for maybe five years now."

The mom rolled her eyes in joy at the item just sampled, "Wow this is . . ." her voice drifting off to chew.

"The other times, there were a lot more items to move," said, Sparky smiling impishly.

In total bliss the mom held out a spoon full of food toward the mother of twins, "Oh, try this."

"We've never cooked for you before, though."

"No, I would remember that, dammit this is good—pardon me" aid the mother of twins looking at the magic spoon full of food that mom continued to hold out for her.

"What is your association with the team, ma'am?" asked Pops respectfully.

"My husband is one of the administrators. I help him with stuff like this sometimes," she said, then looked at the boy's mom, opening her hand to her so that she can introduce herself.

The mom suddenly realized she needed to break out of her food stupor and respond to the introduction. "Oh. I guess my husband is what they call a pinch hitter."

Instantly the three boys froze. Then they sprang to their feet, mouths open in shock, staring at her.

"Shut up!" Said Owl.

"No way!"

"Are you kidding me?" said Red.

"Is he the old guy that's been hitting all those home runs?" said Pops.

The men's reactions stunned the boy's mom. So, the mother of twins answered for her.

"He sure is, and he's a very nice man, would you like to meet him?"

Like rapid fire shotguns the young men responded.

"Heck ya, I would!"

"Damn right!"

"Yes, can you do that?" finished Red.

"I'm pretty sure," said the mother of twins looking at the mom, smiling.

"Holy crap!" said Owl as they all high fived each other.

"We can get you tickets too. Ever watched a game from the luxury box?" said the mother of twins with a big smile.

The young men all went into hyper mode, like groupies about to meet a rock star, and started pulling stuff out of the icebox, cupboards, and previously hidden containers.

"You're in trouble now, ladies," said the Pops watching them and smiling like the Cheshire cat.

Soon the men turned around. "We made this fresh this morning," said Sparky with a proud look on his face.

"This is our pistachio caramel ice cream," continued Owl.

"With chocolate chip cookie crumbles," offered Red as they set it down in front of the mom of the boy.

"The cookies are fresh too," said Owl looking on.

"Hey, what about me? My husband hired him?" said the mother of twins, laughing.

The young men apologized like they stepped on God's toes and quickly produced another bowl for the mother of twins. As they handed it to her, Pops said, "Boys, do you think the children might like some of that chocolate ice cream you got hidden in there?"

"Yes, please!" the twins chimed in unison.

A knock at the cabin door interrupted this fun. Pops rolled down the window, and a voice from outside was heard. "Hey, buddy, I've got a load here, how long you gonna be?"

"I can move it out right now," Pops said and rolled up the window. He turned to the group. "Why don't I drive this over to that parking lot, so this gentleman can conduct his business, and you can finish your lunches. Would that be OK?"

"Sure!"

"Meals on wheels!"

"OK, then everyone, buckle up," he said, shifting. With that, the room started to move away.

WALKED

The dad stood alone in his dark hotel room, watching as the late-night sports show flickered to life.

"Oh, why him? I hate this guy," said the dad as he realized which announcer would be covering tonight's game.

"Hello, folks. Tonight, we are going to show you highlights from what just might be the funniest thing you have ever seen, so stay put, stay right where you are. I promise you, you want to see this!"

"Give me a break, it wasn't so bad," he whispered to himself as the TV continued on.

"First, let us give him his due. He has batted three times in the major leagues, and as you all know that he has hit a home run every, single, time. You can't take that away. Our hats are off to him!"

"All right, that's better, thank you," he said proudly, louder this time.

"But! He has never had to run the bases, and you are in for a treat because tonight he did! He had to run the bases!"

"Oh God! I hate this guy."

"Now you are going to get to see him do that, and it is incredible! This is toooo funny, it's waaay too funny to watch standing up. It's not safe to stand, so please sit down—you might very well faint!"

"Oh no!" he thought as he sat down.

"Did he get some other hit, you ask?"

"No, they walked me, dammit!"

"No, they put him in, hoping that he would hit another home run. Did he?"

"No, they walked m—!"

"And instead, they walked him!"

"They walked me. Why would they do that?" he said, slumping back down, hoping to hide in the cushions of the chair.

"So, there he is standing on virgin ground. Oh, he has tripped over first base a few times but never had to stand on it. And this is where it starts to get good. Look closely, hee-hee. Now look, hee-hee—there! You can see him looking in the dugout? He's expecting a pinch runner. Hee-hee. Now look at his expression, look at that. He ain't gonna get one."

"Should have taken me out, son of a—" he spewed angrily at the TV.

"Apparently the manager either does not like him, or . . . well, I can't imagine any other reason, he must hate him! He made him run the bases, and we all have to thank him for that. Hell, he's my coach of the year for this one act alone!"

"Hate him," he said, even angrier.

"Look how scared he looks, but wait, it gets better."

"There look at that! Is that not the smallest leadoff in the history of baseball? What is that? Twelve inches? Now freeze that. Zoom into his eyes. Look at that! Is that the look of fear or what? The man is absolutely terrified."

"Oh my God! I look terrified. I was terrified, dammit!"

"And then watch this, the pitcher must be in on the joke, because he tries to pick him off!"

"Why? I hate him too!"

"And he basically, hee-hee-hee-hee, he sits down on first base like a toddler in a barber chair, he sits on the base! Ha-ha-ha-ha-ha."

"Why did he do that? Really? Like I would steal? Jerk! God, I hate him!"

"But wait there's more, and it just gets funnier. Hee-hee. The man can hardly get up. He has to use two hands to push himself up! OK, stop the tape. I need to laugh for a second. HAHAHAHAHA. He looks like a giraffe trying to get water."

"I'm old, dammit. You try it."

"OK start it again. But then the unthinkable happens, and he has to actually run, and folks, it's ugly. The next batter rips it down right-field line into the corner."

"No, no, no—"

"An easy double, right? Well, apparently not. Not when it takes the guy in front of you fifteen seconds to run to second base and then when he comes to a full stop to look around! Nobody does that!"

"Oh, this is awful. Just hate. . ."

"But the ball gets by the right fielder, so he has to run more. But he is so slow that even after that they would have had him."

"Oh no, oh my God!"

"He's an easy out, but the throw is wild, and he gets waved home by third-base coach."

"I'm never gonna . . . damn. Look at—"

"Look at the coach; he is laughing his butt off the whole time.

"I'm gonna kill him. He did that on purpose."

"So, there he goes with those short little bowlegs waddling toward home."

"Oh no."

"Glaciers could have easily scored, but he's so slow."

"No!"

"There's going to be a play at the plate!

"Oh no. No, no!"

"Look: it's right out of Charlie Brown. He tries to slide and ends up three feet short. HA-HA-HA-HA-HA-HA-HA-HA-HA-HA-HA-HA!"

"I've never slid in my life, dammit!" he yelled at the screen "This isn't fair!"

"Wait! Replay that! Have you ever seen an uglier slide in your life?"

"Oh, really! Come on!"

"Like a big ole bird crash landing, plop—ugly slide, HAHAHAHAHAHA!"

"Stop it! Oh my. That's awful."

"But wait it's another bad throw, and this just keeps getting better and better. Oh my God folks, I'm so happy, folks, we get to watch replays of this our whole life. This will be remembered forever!"

"Really? Awful."

"So here it is. He tries to get home by scooching feet first on his butt, like a crab or spider or something."

"Oh nooo! Nooo oh! Nooo! That's so . . . my that really is awful. TV really does make you look fat."

"Nobody does that—ever! Ever! Ever! In the history of baseball, nobody has ever tried to score like that."

"Oh my, nooo!"

"Meanwhile, the catcher has run all the way to the backstop and back and dives at him. He landed on top of him just as he finally makes it to home plate.

"Oh no!"

"This was absolutely the funniest thing I've ever seen, and I've already watched this ten times, folks. I'm trying to be a professional here and not cry but HAHAHAHAHA—look at this poor guy! Look at him! Face down—the poor guy can't move; he is absolutely exhausted."

"I was, I was!"

"But wait, here's the best part. Watch carefully. HA-HA-HA-HA-HA-HA-HA. This is it, the crown jewel you've all been waiting for."

"Please don't! Oh, I hate this guy with the passion of . . . "

"Watch, he's moving. He gets up to his hands and knees arches his back, and—HAHAHAHAHAHAHA—he pukes all over home plate. HAHAHAHAHAHAHA!

"Here, watch again! Arch, puke. Arch puke. Arch puke. I'm gonna puke I'm laughing so hard, oh my!"

"Oh my! Oh no!"

"So, come back after the commercial, and I'll show you the rest of what happened—it's even more amazing than what you just witnessed!"

He slumped in his chair as the commercials played. "This is agony," he thought. "I wanna go home." He sat there in his underwear for the next three minutes, considering his bruised body and bony knees. "Why did I slide? Why would anybody slide? It really hurts. That was a lot of puke! I feel bad for that groundskeeper. I should get him flowers."

Suddenly the TV cut in, and he heard the announcer's voice as the show started again. "Welcome back. We pick up, and it is the tenth inning, one on, one out, and the Tigers are down 5–4 and guess who comes back to bat? Yep, that's right, and he's facing the fastest pitcher in the major leagues, and it all ends in three quick pitches. The highlights? Here we go. First pitch, 100 mph fastball . . . strike!"

"Damn! I had no idea. That's fast," whispered the dad.

"Second pitch, 102 mph fastball . . . strike!"

"Damn!"

"Third pitch, 103 mph fastball—yes he did—yes he did! Deep fly ball, way back, and that ball is . . ."

"That right, he did!" he yelled now, and beat his chest. Then, he spoke simultaneously with the announcer:

"Gone!

"He hit over the right-field wall, he was late on it, but managed to catch up enough to squeeze it just inside the foul pole for his fifth home run in a row. Absolutely amazing!

"Folks, we can laugh at this guy all we want, but he is only three home runs away from tying the all-time record for home runs in consecutive games. Think about that for a second. That's such a rare record people don't even talk about it. Folks, there's an old saying, and it goes like this: 'He might not be the best, but the best, best not mess with him.' We can laugh at him all we want, but every single time he has batted, he has had the last laugh. So hats off, sir, keep it up!"

"Damn! I like this guy!"

DREAMS

Was it the fact that the dad was such a ridiculous-looking human being that attracted attention, or might it be his age, or how clearly unathletic he was? Many players were more deserving of the attention he was getting. The reality was that nobody in league history had ever done so well, and at the same time, looked so ridiculous.

He had become huge national news, and everybody wanted to talk to him or make offers to appear on the morning and late-night shows. He did go on Jay Leno, and while he liked Mr. Leno, he hated the experience of being in front of an audience. He stopped accepting offers after that. *Saturday Night Live* did a hilarious skit with long lines of fat guys trying out for various sports or things like the ballet, high jumping, and Olympic events. The scene with the eight fat guys in a rowing scull was particularly hysterical.

The nights after road games were the worst. Too wired to sleep, his mind drifted endlessly as he stared at strange cityscapes that flickered in the dark. Consumed with thoughts of home, his past, and the future, he sat alone. There was no progression leading up to this life, just a sudden change. Had the raffle really done all that? He wanted more of those memories from his old life, but would the future ever be the same again?

He never aspired beyond a man's primary desire for dignity, and there is none when a million eyes judge your every inch. Anonymous crowds deem you unworthy, too short, too bald, too this, too that—all dressed up, lights and cameras, the binary result of every action, a thumbs up or down. His successes accidental, the exhilaration of this experience lost in the reality of weeks of mindless waiting, interrupted by seconds of sheer terror.

Some men are made for battle, some for passive lives. He always admired athletes but never aspired to be one, and had none of the delusions that young men have. No fake conceit, he accepted who he was, and what he was. Youth frees young men to run and jump, lift and work at full speed all day, just as age fills old men with doubts about their ability to do the same. The act of healing once just a shrug, a dull ache now becomes a constant nuisance.

He was happy with his simple life, in his skin, and with his lack of dreams. A man of no importance, he tried to understand why, suddenly, he was living this dream he never had. Not strong, fast, or gifted, why now at forty was he able to beat the young men who were?

People he didn't know wanted things from him, to do things for him, to give him more and more, while all he wanted was less and less. The better he did, the more he felt like an outsider. He was never going to be accepted where he was, and was never going be accepted again where he came from. No longer fully part of either world, participation in one forever excluded him from the other. Home is where acceptance is, and he had not been home in five weeks.

He missed his life, missed his wife, his boy, and his home, and while fancy hotels were great, all he did in them was sit in the dark and dream about being someplace else.

THE THIMBLE RIG

About the same time that P.T. Barnum and Abner Doubleday were getting started with their particular claims to fame, a man named William B. Thornton was becoming very wealthy in the California Gold Rush. The gold he found was not from mining but instead from playing a game of deception called "the Thimble Rig." Lucky Bill Thornton was a tall, broad-shouldered man with curly black hair and large gray eyes. Lucky Bill was a ladies' man and traveled with three lovely young women in an area where ladies were as hard to find as gold nuggets.

Lucky Bill played the game using identical little metal cups and a single cork pea. The action of the game was to place a pea under a cup on a flat surface, and then move around and mix up the cups while the other player watched. The game's premise was that the other player would follow the dancing cups and then pick the one that contained the pea. If the player chose the correct cup, he would win the bet.

However, Lucky Bill was a skilled practitioner in the art of cheating and misdirection. He got them to look one place while hiding the pea somewhere else. He had total control over who won and when. The gamblers that lost their money to Lucky Bill assumed they lost because they failed to follow the cup hiding the pea. The deception was that it was never under any of the cups at all. He used his long fingernails to trap the pea unseen between his nail and finger as he pretended to set a cup down over it. The pea was never under any of the cups until Bill put it back down to show the other player where it was.

The pretty girls would smile and laugh and do the things that women do to get the attention of men, distracting the gamblers, and the crowd, so there was no chance of them seeing either end of Lucky Bill's deception.

Like the Thimble Rig, what happened that day at the ballpark was all about deception. The deception at the ballpark on this day all started because the two principal participants believed they saw and heard something they did not actually see or hear. It began when, with two outs at the bottom of the ninth inning, the dad hit a deep fly ball down the right-field line. The right fielder made a great play to jump above the fence to catch the ball. In doing so, he slammed into the wall with such force that the ball popped out of his glove. Logic would dictate that this ball could only fall one of two places: into the stands, or onto the ground.

The impact disoriented the right fielder, who then landed hard with his back pressed against the soft flesh of the heavily padded outfield wall. He didn't see where the ball went, but he knew that he had not made the catch. Not finding the ball on the ground, he assumed it was a walk-off home run.

At the same time, 325 feet away, the dad saw the fielder leap to catch the ball and that the umpire did not signal home run, so he assumed that he must be out and that the game was over. The chaos of the crowd confirmed for both men what each thought happened.

Upset his failure had ended the game, the fielder started a slow jog back toward his dugout as did most of his teammates. Upset he just had made the last out of the game, the dad dropped his head, and after stepping on the first base, began a slow dejected walk toward second base.

Houdini once said, "What the eyes see and ears hear, the mind believes." The gods of baseball were playing a Thimble Rig game with both men that day, and things were not what they seemed for either man. The gods had in mind a third option for the ball after it popped out of the fielder's mitt. As gravity pulled the ball downward, the fielder unknowingly trapped it between his back and the soft padding of the outfield wall, where it remained a live ball.

Early on during his time with the team, coaches mostly ignored the dad and didn't appear to care what he did. Since he felt out of place and self-conscious, he avoided team workouts and training sessions. He had no idea how to train or do any of the things that the real athletes were doing. And since his body was perhaps the least athletic thing anyone had ever seen, he didn't care to put that on display.

Pretty quickly, the team's trainers had also figured how limited he was. They realized that he had no idea how to physically prepare or improve himself, and started by shaming him into jogging, albeit on a private treadmill. Then they taught him how to breathe, showed him how to lift, stretch, and got him eating an athletic diet. At first, it was drudgery, but now he understood what it felt like to feel good, and he looked forward to his daily supervised workout. He was able to do his versions of wind sprints, laps, and was even working with the team every day. He was still the weakest, slowest, and least coordinated person on the field, but he was much improved from the pathetic specimen who arrived six weeks ago. All that training was an effort to improve his speed and endurance on the base paths in case he ever had a moment like this, because he was very, very slow.

The fastest recorded time for a player running run from home plate to first base is an incredible 3.6 seconds. The average MLB time for the same distance is six seconds, and the boy's dad could now do it in ten seconds. The average time for a Major League Baseball player to run around all the bases is twenty-two seconds. Even with all his new training, it still took the dad a significantly longer time to do it.

As the right fielder moved away from the wall, the trapped ball fell to the ground behind him. The dad was still about twenty feet from second base when he saw the ball sitting there. He realized what had happened and started to run as fast as he could. The center fielder also saw the ball fall and began to run at it from center field, yelling and pointing like a madman as the crowd roared to life.

The oblivious right fielder was startled when he noticed the dad start to suddenly run faster. He began looking around. Then he saw the center fielder sprinting and finally found the ball. Panicked now, the right fielder made a desperate attempt to get to the ball. When he reached for it, he collided with the center fielder, spilling both men to the turf and sending the ball rolling even farther away.

For as long as people have watched sports, there have been arguments about what is the single most exciting play. Lots of plays in football and basketball are exciting, but they are over too quickly, and the best plays in hockey appear out of nowhere, so they lack the buildup required.

Some fans say that the single most exciting play in all of sports is essentially just a race. It involves a player running around the bases and trying to do it faster than the other side can gather up the ball and get it back to home plate. They insist that the most exciting play in all of sports is the inside the park home run!

First, there is the crowd's realization of the play's potential as it begins to unfold. Then there is the question of the runner's speed and endurance and whether the third-base coach has the guts to send him. If he does, there is the beauty of the well-rehearsed relay throws that all must be perfectly executed. Last, will the final catch and tag be matched by an equally artful slide by the runner? Even a fast, inside-the-park home run takes at least twenty-two seconds, so the buildup to the climax is very long and has many moving parts. Then, we all hold our breath and wait for the home plate umpire to make an overly dramatic final call to complete the play.

In this case, the desperate center fielder emerged from his somersault in deep right field and made a perfect throw to the first baseman. He relayed it instantly on the line to the waiting catcher, who slapped a quick tag just as the dad dove headfirst into home plate.

The umpire hovered over home plate, peering into the pile of bodies, waiting for the dust to clear as the crowd held its collective breath. Slowly, the dad rose to his hands and knees, and the crowd erupted as there, beneath him, was the ball, lying on the ground.

WIFFLE BALLS

The Wiffle ball game had changed over time. It had started off as private time where the dad and his son could continue to play, then that turned into a batting practice for one, then three, and then a game for the many. Now it was a full-fledged organized practice that was filmed, involving fifteen players, seven field crew, four trainers, and three coaches. Instead of one bat and three balls, there was now a dedicated golf cart with bins for three different kinds of Wiffle ball bats and barrels for four types of Wiffle balls. There was now a formal home plate and a slick stand behind home plate with a dangling sheet of tin that, when struck by a Wiffle ball, would make a great crashing sound to indicate a strike.

The sheet was divided into nine numbered squares that allowed the batting coach to signal the pitcher which square to aim at. The idea being that they could work on isolating a specific area of weakness a batter might have. This, of course, is predicated on having a pitcher that could actually hit one of those squares repeatedly. So far, none of the batting practice pitchers could hit those squares with a Wiffle ball. Thus, the boy had become a paid batting practice pitcher with a uniform and schedule to keep. They even had a special camera that recorded the grip, arm slot, and attack angle of each ball the boy threw.

The organization thought that the boy would like to have a uniform so he could feel like one of the players. While the gesture was innocent enough, the autistic mind works differently, and the boy was not easily be convinced to wear the uniform. Clothing, like everything else the autistic mind encounters, is extremely specific. In his regular life, the boy wore the same six T-shirts, shorts, and the same three pairs of socks every day. The shirts had to be put on in a particular order. The silky shirt was always against his skin, then a long-sleeve shirt, another silky tee, the red shirt, the blue shirt, followed by two black T-shirts, size XXL. This was not negotiable, it just was the way it was, and despite all conventional logic, it was the way it would always be, autisim always wins.

The first attempt to place a jersey on the boy was met with violent, frightened resistance. A couple of well-meaning players tried to surprise him by trying to pull the jersey over his head without warning. The father quickly came to their rescue when the boy collapsed to the floor, wiggling and spinning wildly as if caught by a boa constrictor trying to shed his skin. The well-meaning men were near tears at his reaction, apologizing as if they had caused the end of the world. The dad just laughed it off as he calmed the boy and welcomed them to the world of autism, explaining to them the reality of the situation.

Eventually, the mom, as was her way, was able to train the boy to wear the jersey using her rules of comfort and proximity. Her strategy was to place the uniform on the side of the boy's bed, then wait for him to get curious. After a few days, the boy started to experiment with it on his own, and eventually, he sought help from her to put it on. Soon, he was wearing it over his other shirts, and it quickly became his new outer skin.

One of the most common mannerisms of autism is the need for repetitive actions, so luckily throwing two hundred Wiffle ball pitches in a row was not a problem for the boy. He used to decide his activity in the morning, but like all people, the boy had lost his freedom of choice. He had become a working stiff like the rest of the team. So far, though, the boy seemed to like doing this, as in the past, he had always just stopped whenever he didn't like doing something. Being interactive with a broad mix of people was probably good for Chad's development, but that didn't change the fact that the dad liked his time with the boy and missed it.

During practice, the batting coach kept going on and on, using catch words like "eye-hand coordination," "repetitive action," or "refinement." He was acting like he invented Wiffle ball as a training technique and was carrying on like he had been doing this for years. He had recently appeared on TV shows, teaching "his techniques," and claiming credit for the team's recent batting average improvement.

All this was to sell his line of training videos, each centered around the use of Wiffle ball as a training aid. He was also now signing his own range of Wiffle ball equipment that he called signature bats, balls, and the numbered sheet of tin. He even reinvented the Wiffle ball, offering different versions with different hole patterns said to curve or respond in bigger and better ways. One of his signature inventions he called "the Reduction Series" of balls. These were just balls that got progressively smaller in size. The theory was that as a hitter mastered one of the larger sizes, he would move to the next size down to further refine his skill. The coach gave each sized ball its own fancy name. The full size was called the Amateur, the three-quarter size was named the Dude, the half size was titled the Pro, and finally, the one-quarter size was given the grandiose name the HOF after the Hall of Fame. This made the ball harder to hit, and it allowed the pitcher to throw it much faster with tighter curves. For Major Leaguers, that was actually a good thing.

The coach's name was also starting to be mentioned as a candidate for head coaching jobs around the league. Most appalling, he was taking credit for taking a forty-year-old nobody and turning him into a home-run hitter.

The dad was very uncomfortable with this self-promotion, so he had stopped participating in these practices, using the excuse that he was injured. Instead, he sat in the stands with the mom and watched. Nobody understood how he was doing the things he did, so the overall strategy was to stay out of his way and not mess with him.

On the whole, though, the batting coach had become outwardly a much happier person. He was saying outrageous things like please and thank you to total strangers and generally treating people nicely. At first, those who knew him took this for sarcasm. But soon people had bought into it and liked the new him. He always made a point of warmly greeting the mom and shook the boy's hand at the start and end of every practice, making sure to thank him by name loud enough for others to hear. And now, he always looked the dad in the eyes, nodded his head respectfully, and warmly said thank you.

TIPPING

I t had been seven weeks since the dad won that raffle,. He had batted only six times, but it felt like he had watched a thousand games and millions of at bats. He was perched in his usual spot at the far end of the bench as he watched this game and was kind of bored with the whole thing. Technically, though, he was a highly paid Major League ballplayer, so he did his best to act interested. He chewed on an endless supply of sunflower seeds and spit the pieces in an ever-thickening carpet of bits in front of him. He used the time between pitches to spit chunks of seeds at a specific stain on the filthy dugout floor. Occasionally, a spit wad would get close to the mark, and in that small achievement, he found some relief from the endless monotony of the time between actual action on the ballfield. Near hits were infrequent; most of the time his seeds would sail far from the mark.

The game he was watching today was far closer than most games as the score was only 1–0. To him, it was also more boring than most games. Both pitchers today were dominant, so not much had happened. While baseball purists love these kinds of close, pitching-dominated games, the boy's dad found it rather mind numbing. Today's opposing pitcher was considered one of the greats of the game, and the dad understood that it was supposed to be exciting. But for him, watching a great pitcher do his thing was like watching a train go down the tracks: a marvel to watch, incredibly powerful, awe inspiring, but after a while, just an endless string of the exact same thing. If you just look down the tracks, it's pretty clear where you're going to end up—

no surprises in either direction. Nothing is ever different; it's all the same. Today this man was especially great, and by the sixth inning, he had given up only one hit using just sixty-five pitches.

Then, like a lightning bolt, it hit him. The dad noticed that the pitcher did something different, and a few pitches later, he saw him do it again. Pitchers mask what kind of pitch they are going to throw by trying to do everything exactly the same on every throw right up to the instant they release the ball. If they do this correctly, it makes it very difficult for the hitters to know what pitch is coming because they all look the same. If pitchers do things slightly different for each pitch, hitters can figure out what type of ball is coming. This is called "tipping your pitches." Most teams put quite a bit of effort watching for a pitcher tipping his pitches, because knowing what kind of ball is coming is a game-changer at the Major League level.

The dad watched another couple of batters just to confirm what he was seeing, and then he told the pitching coach.

The boy's dad had noticed that when this pitcher threw his fastball, there was a slight pause before he came to the plate, and when he threw a curve, the pause was not there. The pause was very short, a fraction of a second, just a hitch, really, but once he noticed it, he couldn't help but see it. This tiny tip had great potential for a good hitter to take advantage of.

"Prove it!" said the coach.

In the eighth inning, the dad predicted every single pitch, and that was proof enough. Between innings, the batting coach talked with the manager. As the two men talked, they looked sideways at him like he was some deviant criminal who had stolen cake from a baby. When the huddle ended, the manager took a long, slow walk, head down, toward him. The manager stopped just in front of the dad but then turned away and looked out at the field for what seemed like hours. Finally, he turned toward the dad, stared at him for several seconds, and said: "You sure?"

The dad just nodded, looking right back at him.

"You really sure?" There was a long pause as the two men

continued to look at each other.

"Why should I trust you?"

Again the dad didn't answer but just stared back, eye to eye, privately finding the manager's approach rather comical.

"OK then. If someone gets on base in the ninth, then you're gonna bat next; if they don't, you're gonna bat last."

Up to this point, the pitcher had given up just two soft hits and had only thrown ninety pitches, so he got the call to finish the game. The first batter of the inning managed to hit a weak little "nubber," an accidental slow roller down the third-base line that ended up being impossible to defend, so he made it to first base safely.

With a runner on first base, the dad headed out to bat with the score 1–0. When he played Wiffle ball with his kid, the dad found it easiest to hit curveballs, so he had made up his mind to wait for one, since he could now tell when one was coming. But so far, no one had ever thrown him a Major League curveball. What the dad didn't realize was that a Wiffle ball curve and a Major League curve are entirely different animals. From a right-handed pitcher, the Wiffle floats as it curves right to left, while the Major League curve drops sharply from top to bottom.

But before he could get out of the dugout, the manager stopped him and said:

"Tell me your plan, what are you gonna do?"

"I'm gonna wait and hit the curve!"

"You sure? Fastballs go farther, easier to hit . . . ?"

The dad just stared back at him.

"Nobody hits a good curveball."

"OK."

"Dammit. Are you sure?" boomed the coach as if expecting a guarantee.

"Coach, really? I've been doing this seven weeks; I've batted, what, six times, maybe eight times my whole life? I'm not sure of anything! I still can't believe you ever let me hit at all. What were you thinking, coach?" said the dad with a big grin.

These two strangers had no understanding of each other's worlds and stood there looking at each other, like the man before them had an undiscovered species of bug crawling on his face. The dad finally blurted out: "You want me to go hit or what?" He motioned toward the field with his bat.

"OK, you're right. Your plan—it's yours, go do it, goddammit!" the coach said, swatting the dad on his butt and pushing him out onto the field.

The dad had decided he would watch the first pitch just to get a feel for the pitcher's rhythm. He watched the first pitch, and there it was, a hitch, and he let a fastball sail by for a strike. He saw the hitch right away on the second pitch and let it go by for a strike as well. Again, there was a hitch for the third pitch, but he could tell it was going to be outside, so he did not swing at it—the pitcher was trying to get him to swing at a bad pitch. Finally, on the fourth pitch, there was no hitch.

People new to baseball always ask: "How do you hit a good curveball?"

The answer is: "You don't."

Batters that hit curveballs don't swing at the good ones, they only swing at the bad ones.
In the pantheon of baseball pitches, a curveball is one of many balls that breaks or curves down as it comes to the plate. Splitters, fork balls, sliders, slurves, and screwballs all break down, and each has its own trait or particular tail at the end of the flight path. The curve, though, is the king of the breaking pitches and has the biggest drop of all.

When a curve is coming in lower than belt high, it is a good curveball, and it breaks down out of the strike zone at the last second. A good hitter knows that if he swings at and hits a good curveball, the best that can happen is that he will hit a ground ball. Most of the time, batters swing and miss at good curveballs.

However, when a curve is coming in above the belt, it is going to be a "hanging curveball." A hanging curve is a pitch that is easy to hit, and it can be hit hard and far. The dad didn't know any of that; he just knew a curveball was coming, and that he was going to swing at it.

When a player hits his first Major League home run, it is baseball tradition that his teammates will look the other way as he runs around the bases. They are not there to greet him when he steps on home plate, and even when he returns to the dugout, they all act like nothing happened and completely ignore him. After every home run since his first one, though, there had always been at least a few teammates at home plate to greet the dad. Today he rounded third base and headed for home and standing in line to shake his hand was the manager, followed by the batting coach.

NICE DAY

The ladies were walking in the exact same spot where, in November of 1906, Harry Houdini allowed himself to be trapped in chains from head to foot and jumped off the Belle Isle bridge into the frigid waters of the Detroit River. It was a stunt that would elevate him to legendary status among escape artists. A great fiction of that event is that Houdini broke through the ice to perform the feat beneath it. It turns out things are not always as they seem. There is no evidence that there was ice on the river that day, but lack of ice does not diminish the danger of his feat. When asked later how he was able to escape from those chains, he responded: "What the eyes see, and ears hear, the mind believes."

But this was August, and it was a beautiful day at Belle Isle Park, and the ladies were enjoying the walk with the three kids who skittered ahead of them, searching for stones or sticks to throw into the river. Belle Isle is a beautiful thousand-acre park located in the middle of the Detroit River just off the coast and is connected to the city by the bridge that they were now walking on. The topic that day was small and unimportant, as the point of the walk was to enjoy the company of friends, the sunshine, and the beauty of Belle Isle.

"Has he got used to being a Major League Baseball player yet?" asked the mother of twins, shielding her eyes from the sun.

"He doesn't think of himself like that, so no."

"I'm surprised." The mother of twins stopped for a second to look at the mom, then continued on.

"He's still pretty overwhelmed by it. Me too." The mom looked back and tilted her head, smiling.

"Give him time."

"Does he have time? We keep thinking every day is the last."

"He's doing great."

"Is he?"

"At the pace he's going, he might be able to stay quite a while!" Said mother of twins smiling with confidence at the mom.

"I'm not sure he wants to." Said the mom with a shrug.

Sensing it was time to change topics, the mother of twins moved on. "The boy seems to like being here." In the distance, the three kids were holding hands and walking single file on a crack in the pavement as if they were tightrope walkers and the crack was stretched over the river itself.

"I think he does. He has friends here." She meant the two girls.

"But not at home?" puzzled the mother of twins.

"No, the kids at home stay away." Said the mom with a a big exhale.

There was a long pause. "That's hard, huh?"

"Ya." She fought back a tear and glanced away a bit from the conversation.

The kids stepped off the bridge ahead of their mothers and ran down the grassy hill toward the water. They bent down at the water's edge to explore. The ladies stopped just up the hill from them and sat on the hill to watch and continue the conversation.

"Look at him, rolling around in the grass with them. What fun."

"Ya."

"He's a homebody—this is such a big change."

"I bet."

"Says he feels like a fraud."

"Fraud? He's hit, what, six or seven home runs in a row?

Nobody does that, ever! He's doing fantastic!"

"Says he's lucky."

"He is! But luck is kind of an understatement—after a while, it quits being luck and becomes something else."

Suddenly there was a gust of wind that caused the water to ripple more distinctly. The boy stood up unexpectedly at the water's edge and started flipping his hand at the water. Instantly the two girls stood up and imitated him and both ladies stopped talking to watch. As the wind died back down, the boy settled with it and crouched back down and resumed splashing in the water.

"I've always wondered why he does that," said the boy's mom.

"What do the doctors say?"

"They don't have an answer; they just say it's normal."

The two women were silent for a long time as they enjoyed the day. Then the mom turned and asked, "Is it really that good? What he's done?"

"It's great! Amazing, fantastic!" She then paused to think about how to best explain the significance to someone not knowledgeable about baseball. "Did you know I was an athlete?" said the mother of twins, shielding her eyes from the sun as she looked toward the mom.

"No."

"Yep. I played college softball, I mean."

"I didn't know."

"It's different, I know, but I was really good, and I never hit six home runs in a whole season. There are probably seven hundred players in the major leagues right now, and half of them haven't hit seven home runs all season."

"So, he's good?"

"Well, no! He's not! Not as an athlete. I look at him, and I don't see an athlete. I don't know how it's possible for him to do what he has done. That's what's odd: he's not good, his swing is terrible, and yet he does great things, spectacular, unheard of, impossible things!"

The boy's mom laughed. "So how is he doing this?"

"There's no logic to it, and that's what makes it so magical, people love what he's doing because hes one of them. And they love the way he's doing it too. It's really special."

The mother of twins then paused a minute to think before continuing on.

"Is he happy?"

"No, I guess not." The mom stopped herself and looked at her friend. "He really isn't."

"Are you?" asked the mother of twins.

"Yes, I actually am, I kind of love it." They both chuckled.

"Why not? I mean him, why doesn't he like it?"

"It's just not him." A little frustration crept into her voice.

"How so?"

"I guess it's just not his world. He's only doing it because I kind of made him, for the money. It's a lot of money."

"I know, it's insane, are you enjoying that part at least?"

"I'm enjoying all of it! We haven't had the chance to spend very much yet, but we will."

"Well, we should do some of that."

"That sounds fun. He just wants to escape, go back home. He feels trapped, stuck."

"He could just quit."

"Really? Do people do that?"

"No, I guess not."

They sat quietly for a while, watching the kids happily trying to skip stones in the choppy waters of the Detroit River.

"This is such a beautiful day," said the boy's mom, leaning back to soak up the sun.

"Well, it would be if my girls didn't throw like girls. No, this will not do!" said the twins' mom, laughing as she rose to her feet. "It looks like it's time for me to teach my girls how to skip a stone properly." And with that, she started moving toward the water, calling back over her shoulder. "Your little guy's gunna be a pitcher one day . . . he has a great arm!"

TAPE JOB

"Welcome, folks. I am told some of you have just joined this broadcast from our sister networks, so welcome, we've got a good one going on here! We are here in Detroit, where the Mets are in town for an interleague game. Here's what we are looking at. It is the ninth inning of a 1–1 game, and something very remarkable has been going on for the last fifteen minutes.

"Let me set the stage for you. First, he is attempting to extend his own record for consecutive home runs to an incredible eight and simultaneously, to tie the Major League record for consecutive games with a home run, also at eight, a record held by Hall of Famers Ken Griffey Jr., Don Mattingly, and Dale Long.

"As you look at him in the on-deck circle, you should know that he has been at bat for the last sixteen minutes, and you are joining us mid-at-bat after the eighteenth pitch. Yes, I said that right, eighteen pitches in one at bat. If that sounds like a lot, it is. It's the new Major League record for most pitches in one at bat, beating the old record of seventeen by just one pitch, so far.

"Now I only have time to tell you this because we are in the middle of a pitching change! The starter made it to the ninth inning with a pitch count of 110 and came back out, hoping to get three quick outs. Instead, here we are eighteen pitches later, and we are witnessing a very rare mid-at-bat pitching change. Quite honestly, I've been in broadcasting for twenty-four years, and I've never seen that happen before except for injuries. This change, however, is not because of an injury, it is out of necessity. After 128 pitches, the pitcher just decided enough was enough and asked to be taken out.

"The average Major League at bat is just 3.6 pitches long; usually by that time, a batter is out or on base. We are at eighteen and counting, so while the new guy warms up, let me tell you what you've missed.

"Among the eighteen pitches, he has made contact with an incredible twelve balls in a row. There were a lot of foul tips, a few line drives, and two very long foul flies. One of those just missed being a home run by a few inches.

"Finally, we are ready to go with a brand-new pitcher with a fresh arm, and here we go with the nineteenth pitch. And it's a fastball, a good one fouled off behind the screen. That was a defensive swing. It looked like he had him, just got a tiny bit on that one. That was a nice bit of hitting—caught up to it just in time, though.

"Folks, this will be pitch number twenty. I'm told by my statistician that including pitching change, this at bat has taken twenty minutes so far, and that too is another Major League record! ...

"He kicks, deals hard shot foul down the third-base line ... foul ball ... boy, that was close! That didn't sound right I bet he broke his bat on that one. I have to say this is a very impressive at bat. Some of the criticism I've heard about this guy is that he has been lucky a lot. And, while that may be true, there is nothing lucky about this at bat. This is a grind-it-out, working-man's, professional at bat.

"Oh, it looks like he got hurt on that one. Ooh, you can see it in the replay, the ball was in on his fist, and the ball ... went off his hand. Ouch! To hit a line drive that hard, right off your hand, that's gotta hurt!

"Yep, that is clearly broken." An image of his hand appeared on the jumbotron, and there was a collective ew from the crowd. The fingernails on the two largest fingers had been ripped up grotesquely, and at least one of his fingers was bent at an odd angle.

"He might have to sit down. I don't know how he can hit with that. That has to be broken. Ouch, it's really bent, may be dislocated. Either way, that has to hurt."

On the jumbotron, the crowd could see the trainer working with him. The manager walked up to see what was going on, followed by the umpire who recoiled at what he saw.

"So here . . . is the trainer going to . . . ? Oh no, folks, if you're squeamish, you don't want to watch this. It looks like they're gonna reset it right there on the field."

The dad's face appeared on the screen, stoic about what the trainer was doing; he hardly reacted.

"Gone are the days of the odd scared little man I first saw bat eight weeks ago. This guy is all business, his face is the face of a warrior, hardened, dirty, dripping sweat, a distant stare, a real badass."

On the jumbotron, the crowd could see the manager and the umpire watching. The manager looked at the dugout and raised his right hand to indicate he wanted a right-handed pinch hitter.

"I can tell you from personal experience that resetting a dislocation is incredibly painful, there is no way that he's gonna be able to finish this at-bat. Looks like they got a batter over there picking up a bat and putting on a helmet."

Just as the replacement came out of the dugout, the boy's dad yelled loud enough to be heard all over the stadium.

"No!" he shouted and pointed to the dugout.

"Wow. I think he told him to go sit down. Folks, that is a man's man right there. Wow. he is one tough hombre, so that must mean he's staying!"

The camera zoomed in while the trainer jerked the dad's finger out and then pushed it back in the socket. On the jerk, there was a collective squeal of protest from the stands that lingered for several seconds, and then another louder, longer one each time a fingernail was ripped off. The manager and umpire looked like they were going to gag, and one started for the dugout, the other back to the plate, as the trainer finished taping the dad's fingers.

"It's looking to me like he thinks he's going to try and bat. Folks, that would be incredible. I've seen some of the toughest men in baseball history sit down immediately with injuries not half this bad, yet that's what he's going to do—he's going to hit. OK, well, we'll see how this goes.

"Looks like we are all set again, from the windup, he kicks, deals . . . line shot foul, back, he ripped it foul down the third base line. Oh no, that had to hurt, you can see the pain. I have to tell you, folks, this is really an incredible display of toughness here.

"This next pitch will be the twenty-second pitch, here it is . . ." *Crack.*

"Deep fly ball, way back, if it stays fair . . . foul ball, he hit it a mile but just pulled it foul. This is incredible, look at this! In both dugouts, every single person is standing! You don't see that. These guys have seen it all, it takes something extraordinary to get two entire teams standing."

"What now? It looks like—does he need something? Oh no, the trainer is coming back out.

"OK, well, it looks like they're just cutting the tape from those fingers. I guess it hurts more with it on, so he's gonna try it without it. Why not, right?

"Look at him, he is drenched in sweat, literally beat to hell, pardon my French, but I'm a little emotional right now this is one of the most courageous things I've ever seen—what a warrior.

"OK, we are ready to go. This will be the twenty-third pitch. Here's the windup, deals, and oh! Just got a piece of it, but he's still alive.

"Wow look at that!" The camera panned the stands. "I've been doing this job for a very long time, and I have seen an awful lot of ball games, and with the exception of World Series games, I don't think I have ever seen an entire stadium standing during an at bat." Slowly a rhythm started to build throughout the stadium as the standing crowd began to clap in unison leading up to the next pitch.

"Incredible, listen to that. This misfit of a man who on the surface would appear to have no right to ever walk on a professional baseball field has got a stadium full of fans spontaneously clapping in unison for him.

"He steps back into the batter's box, and one more time looks out as the pitcher prepares to throw. Look at that—those fingers are straight up, he can't even grip the bat.

"Here's the pitch." *Crack.* "Deep fly ball, center field, drifting back, back, looking up ... gone! He did it! He did it! He did it! Look at that! He has just tied the Major League record for most consecutive home runs."

The announcer was silent as the image on the screen followed the dad as he started his run around the bases. His head was down, his pace fast and strong. He had the look of an old pro who had done it hundreds of times.

"Eight weeks ago, he could hardly jog to first base, today he's looking strong, and he's gonna touch 'em all! In an amazing at bat that took two pitchers and a record twenty-four pitches. During an at-bat that lasted a record thirty-two minutes, he extends his own record and ties another, and with a broken hand joins the ranks of Ken Griffey Jr., Don Mattingly, and Dale Long as coholder of one of baseball's most coveted records." As this was said as he arrived at home plate and was mobbed by players from both teams.

"Look at that! Even the pitcher slapped him on the back. Folks, I've officially seen it all."

ELWOOD BAR
AND GRILL

On the cold day in 1906 when Houdini jumped into the frigid waters of the Detroit River, he hired a ten-year-old boy from a local neighborhood to help him with the trick. Before diving, he showed the crowd in attendance a set of heavy iron chains with thick padlocks designed to trap him under the freezing waters. Before that, however, he showed that young boy how to hide those chains at just the right time when Houdini distracted the crowd. Instead, Houdini put on and wore fake chains when he actually made the escape. That ten year-old grew up to be a man named Abe Bernstein.

Years after Houdini's escape, when the Purple Gang was at the height of its power in Detroit, the gang appeared from the outside to have no single acknowledged leader. However, insiders all knew that the real leader was Abe Bernstein. In that role, he amassed vast personal wealth. His understanding of the power of deception, which Mr. Houdini taught him, played a significant role in that. When Prohibition ended in 1933, he realized he needed a way to make his wealth look legit, and to that end, sought to build legitimate ways to generate more and hide the money he already had.

In 1936 he decided to construct a building that is now known as the Elwood Bar and Grill. Designed for a corner lot, it is a lovely example of the art moderne or streamline style of architecture. It is a long, thin single-story building that features an original exterior of cream and teal enamel with horizontal silver accents, and it remains that way to this day. It sat in the same location for almost sixty years until the Detroit Tigers organization decided to build Comerica Park in the footprint of where the Elwood Bar was standing. So badly did the Tigers organization desire that exact location for their new stadium that they actually paid to have the Elwood building picked up and moved to its current location a couple of blocks from where it originally stood.

Later in life, Abe Bernstein became a close associate of Jimmy Hoffa's. Given the bar's gangland lineage, speculation was rampant among the construction workers moving it that they would find not only Hoffa's body, but also the Lindbergh baby, buried treasure, or at least a buried safe or two. Alas, none were found, and the Elwood Bar and Grill is now ideally situated on the corner directly across from Comerica Park and Ford Field, the home of the Detroit Lions. It has become a de facto home for pro athletes looking for a meal near the stadium when the crowds aren't around.

Almost three hundred years earlier, an Italian boss named Giovanni Battista Pamphilj commissioned the Spanish painter Diego Velázquez to paint a portrait of him. Mr. Pamphilj was pope at the time, so the commission was a high honor for the painter, and many respected art historians considered the end result, a painting titled *Portrait of Pope Innocent X,* the greatest portrait of all time.

It is painted in a highly realistic style that details the fleshy quality and ruthless nature of the man and the extravagant excess of his office. It depicts a middle-aged man sitting on a throne. He appears to be intelligent and powerful, with eyes that seem to burn right through the soul of any man who dares to challenge him or even just look at the portrait.

Almost three hundred years later, in the year 1954, an artist named Francis Bacon began to produce a series of paintings that have come to be known as the Pope Series. These paintings are all clearly inspired by the work of Velázquez and specifically *Portrait of Pope Innocent X.* In contrast to Velázquez, Bacon's art is expressionist and aims to capture the inner emotions of the man, rather than his realistic exterior. The paintings are fiendish depictions of tortured souls, perhaps showing the same pope chained to his throne for eternity, unable to escape, trapped in hell, raging with open maw at his eternal fate of perpetual pain. The paintings are emotional and frightening images that capture the passion, explosive rage, and hopeless quality of the man. The culmination of Bacon's series is his painting *Figure with Meat.*

When the rest of the world sees an angry man, they see Diego Velázquez's version of the portrait of Pope Innocent X. They see the outside, the skin, hair, and facial features—all the obvious stuff. When the boy sees the same angry man, he sees that too. But additionally, he can see the Francis Bacon's version of the man, the *Figure with Meat* version, the vile, disgusting, Dorian Gray alternative that rips off the flesh to expose the ugly, vicious rage and the deep hate inside him.

The Elwood Bar and Grill was so darn convenient that the dad and the boy had taken to eating there almost every day during their time in the major leagues. The atmosphere was friendly, the food was excellent, and the location was perfect.

On this beautiful Saturday morning, they had just paid for their meal and were walking toward the exit when the boy froze and then suddenly, as if under attack by demons, began to spastically flail about in an effort to escape some unseen presence. In his panic, the boy turned and frantically scrambled behind his dad before falling to his knees, hugging his father's leg as tightly as possible. In the process, the boy knocked over a full table of food, spilling the contents onto a family of diners that were happily eating just seconds before.

The dad had never seen the boy react like this and had no idea what was causing it. He desperately tried to apologize to the room and settle him down, but the boy refused to release his death grip, and all efforts just made him hold on tighter. The entire restaurant was standing now; all eyes were fixed on the terrified boy, recoiling at the sight of his face locked in an endless silent scream. Panicking, the desperate manager gently whispered, "Maybe the boy would be more comfortable outside?"

The boy finally allowed the dad to pick him up and carry him toddler style toward the door. As they approached the door, the boy hugged his dad tighter and tighter. Suddenly the dad noticed his teammate, the hotshot, backup shortstop from Florida, sitting at a table next to the door. Sitting with him was the headhunting pitcher, Goliath. He stopped and looked awkwardly at each for a second, thinking he should say something profound. Instead, he could only utter, "I'm sorry about this." The men nodded blankly at him, and he quickly continued on. Unnerved by the moment, something told the dad to look back, and as he did, he was chilled to see the two men looking at him with eyes that seemed to burn right through him.

The boy looked, too, but instead saw faces locked in a blind and shameless rage. The faces swelled a hundred times in size and moved at him. Gray, dead faces, like *Guernica,* drenched in pain, hovered over the boy, straining at chains to reach him. Fists clenched, ripping flesh from bloody bone, and gaping maws spewed filthy bile at him through jagged teeth. Cowering at the horrible visages of these voracious, self-appointed gods and their withering hate, the boy squeezed his eyes tightly in the hope that they would go away and focused blindly on the rhythm of his father's footsteps.

HATE

Though boy was acting odd that day and refused to take part in the Wiffle ball practice. Instead, he leaned against the wall in the right-field corner, flicking his hand and moving his shoulders in an endless, slow rhythm, shoulders shifting right to left like a scared elephant warning a stranger in its path. These vibrations were new to the boy, and he didn't understand them.

The two men had just finished running sprints. Today was an off day, but as long-time teammates, it was their habit to work out every day. The Wiffle ball practice was happening over in the right-field corner, and as it did, the men were doing post-practice stretching on the grass in left field. Both were solid, but not spectacular, professional baseball players, and both had undeniably earned their place in the league.

From his protected spot, the boy watched those left-field shadows with a sense of dread. One was his friend, and while he knew the other, it had a new, very dark quality to it.

The tall man was the older of the two and had been in the league for about ten years. He grew up on the West Coast and played his college ball at Long Beach State, where he got a degree in criminal justice and played on the team that won back-to-back national championships. During that time, he met his wife, married, and together they had their first child while he was still at the university.

He was an outfielder who had recently become pretty good at hitting curveballs and had made it part of his training routine to have the boy pitch batting practice with the Wiffle ball for at least a few minutes every day. Through that, he had become friends both with dad and boy, and enjoyed their company inside the Wiffle ball environment and out.

The boy could see the darkness look at him. Each time the man would look in his direction, or at his dad, his face would grow huge, magnified as if just inches away, allowing an intimate view of its bubbling emotional bile.

The other player was Florida born and raised. He was a hotshot high school shortstop. He was drafted right out of high school and went straight to the minor leagues, where it took him six years to finally make the Major League roster as a utility infielder. Both were family men who enjoyed fishing and hunting with each other in the off-season. Each had a wife and a couple of kids about the same age as the boy. They had been talking about nothing while they stretched, but then the tone of the conversation became uncomfortable for the tall man.

"He is actually a nice guy—have you talked with him?" He was taken aback by the tone of his friend.

"No. Look at him, he's a joke. He should not be here!" The disdain was palpable as the shortstop watched the Wiffle ball game. As he spoke, he took the time to enunciate every syllable of "should not be here."

At first, the tall man thought his friend was joking, but it occurred to him that this might be something more. "Really? Why not?" he said.

"I just don't like him. He shouldn't be here." As he said this he continued to stare in the uninterrupted fixed gaze of a hunter looking for a weakness.

The boy could see the face as if standing right next to it. It was the essence of hate, and the boy recoiled when this ghastly image grimaced at him. This bully was not at all dull or lifeless, but made of billowing clouds of gray shards squeezing blisters of hate from every pore of his face.

Realizing this wasn't a game, the tall man was becoming genuinely concerned about the tone of his friend. "You're kidding, right?"

The shortstop then looked at his tall friend and shook his head no for greater emphasis. "I'm telling ya, he doesn't belong."

Clenched teeth suddenly emerged and snarled at the boy, causing him to turn away, as frothy puss dripped from sores where the angry lips should be.

"OK, but based on what?"

"He's a joke." He was angry now, clenching his teeth.

"Ya, but he's also got four Major League records already, and he's only batted eight times." The tall man was incredulous at his friend's anger.

"He's a joke."

"That joke has more than you do, or me for that matter."

"He's a joke."

"Ya, you've said that six times, but what about the six game-winning home runs he's hit?" This, of course, just made his friend angrier.

"Fuck you."

"Well, he did." The tall man laughed, not yet realizing the depth of what is going on here.

"Fuck you, he's a joke."

"You're serious?" He was stunned at the shortstop's anger.

"Look at him. he shouldn't be here." The shortstop's teeth were still clenching.

"You keep saying the same stuff over and over, and yet all he does is hit home runs." There was a long pause at this point as both men watched the Wiffle ball game.

The boy could see them pause and the evil face swelled at him, sniffing, drooling like a dog scraping at a squirrel's hole. He could hear the stadium crackle with the sounds of crispies sparking with the groans of hate.

The conversation had become very uncomfortable as the older man tried to understand what was driving his friend's clearly fully developed hatred.

"Every time he bats, it turns into some big deal. Enough already."

"Right, and every time he bats, it's a big deal!"

"It's always some long, drawn-out thing—he turns it into a circus."

"So, what? He hits home runs."

"It's not right!"

"Results, man, this league is about results." He was getting loud now and growing frustrated with his friend's rage at the man he knew to be a kind, friendly family man.

The boy was becoming overwhelmed with this imagery that he did not understand, and the bombardment had weakened him, causing him to slump before sitting on the ground.

"But look at him." Said the shortstop holding out his hands as if it must be obvious to all.

"You look at him. What's your problem with his looks? This is stupid." As he said this, he dipped his head and lifted his eyes like a schoolmarm interrupted by an annoying child.

"It's just not right. He just shows up out of the blue, and suddenly, he's on the team?"

"I'll give you that." He nodded in agreement. "But what has he done wrong while he is here?" The tall man was speaking in a quiet tone now.

"He shouldn't be here at all. Why don't you get it?"

"You keep saying that, but why?" Chuckled the tall man.

"He's not one of us. This isn't just some club."

Almost in a whisper, and shaking his head in disbelief, the tall man said, "That's exactly what it is.'

"It's for the elite."

A dread appeared in the back of the tall man's mind. "The elite?"

"Like us, he's not elite."

He grew calm as he tried to drill down and discover the depths of his friend's thoughts. "Why, what more does he need to do?"

"We all had to be drafted, we all had to work for it."

"He just took a different path, look at the results. C'mon, you're just jealous." Said the tall man now laughing at him again.

"Of what?"

"You have three dingers all season. He has eight home runs in eight at bats. He gets all the press."

"Go to hell!" Furious now, he was yelling, his rage building as this went on.

"You're jealous," laughed the tall man even louder now.

"Go to hell!" The shortstop raged.

"You are, you're jealous."

"It's not frickin' fair!" His anger and volume built.

"What does fair have to do with it!" Yelled the tall man back at him.

"I spent six years in the minors," exploded the shortstop, red-faced.

"Me too, we all did." The tall man matched him in anger.

"Not him, he never played a game in the minors, he's not —"

"Ready? He seems pretty ready so far." Said the tall man cutting him off like a teacher talking to a petulant student.

"It is not fair." Shot back the shortstop loudly.

"Based on what he's doing, maybe nobody should be in the minors."

"It's not fair."

"Dude, you gotta give it up."

The boy shut his eyes and dropped his head between his legs, trying to block it out.

Again, there was a pause as the shortstop stopped to consider what had just been said to him. The two men looked at each other for several seconds.

The boy could hear the sounds of sloshing pus grow still, wet waves of hate coagulating like concrete puddles, the monster's feet trapped in a pause, if just for now.

"Go to hell." Said the shortstop a a hushed tone that was creepy for its lack of emotion.

"He really is a nice man." Whispered back the tall man.

"So is my dad." The shortstop paused briefly to gather his thoughts.

"Listen, I get it, he hit a few home runs, but it cheapens the game, and makes us all look bad when this dude comes in and starts hitting home runs like it's no big deal."

Loud and even violent arguments between elite athletes like these men were not at all unusual. These men were the predators, the warriors of our society, and sports had replaced the need for predators and the intimacy of battle and given the predators something else to do beside wage war on the rest of us. Athletes can move quickly from a resting state to battle mode and back. They remain unstressed by being in the state of fury one second and resting calmly the next. They are genetically wired for and well trained to take maximum advantage of a fury state of mind. These two men had argued many times; the act of yelling at each other was as normal as breathing in and out. The topic, however, was not, but for now, things were quiet again.

"I wish I could hit home runs as easily as he does." Mused the tall man.

"He doesn't even play in the field." Shot back the shortstop.

"Neither do the fifty other designated hitters in the league."

"He's taking jobs away from more deserving guys."

"He only bats once a week. What's your problem?"

"He acts all superior to us." Said the shortstop glaring in the direction of the Whiffle ball game.

"How so?" Asked the puzzled tall man.

"Always off by himself, always avoiding the rest of the team."

"He's afraid of us. Just look at him." The tall man offered hoping to offer reassurances.

"You look at him."

"This is stupid! He is no threat to you. Why does this bother you so much?"

"It's just wrong. The man doesn't know anything about baseball."

"And yet he hits home runs."

"He needs to just stay away from me." Said the shortstop through clenched teeth.

"You know if you would take the time to talk to him—"

"Not a chance. And what's with that kid of his?" Now dripping distain and disgust from every pore.

The boy jumped to his feet and ran to where his father was, trying to hide behind him.

"Don't go there." Threatened the tall man shaking his head from side to side.

"Walks around, drooling all the time. What an idiot."

"Don't go there." The tall man was getting mad now.

"Must not be very good parents. The kid can't even talk."

"Don't go there. You're kidding, right? Tell me you're kidding." Demanded the tall man.

"Well, what's up with him? I'll tell you what."

"Don't say it."

"Fucking piece of—I wouldn't let my kid play with him."

"Oh no."

"I don't want my kid to catch it."

"Catch what? It is called autism, and it's not something you can catch, you're born with it."

"I'm not taking chances with my kids." The shortstop was preaching now, lost in a cloud of hate entirely of his own making.

"It's not contagious." Offered the tall man as if in call and response as the shortstop preached on.

"My kids are perfect."

"Must be nice?"

"Fuck you—they are."

"He is a very nice boy, sweet."

"Look at him, he's goofy. Keep him away from my kids."

"He is autistic! Do you understand what that means?"

"It means he better stay out of my way."

"Oh c'mon."

"Not with my kids. Why does he get to hang around here, anyway?"

"You're making me sick."

"As far as I'm concerned, he shouldn't be allowed in our locker room."

"Should he have his own locker room?"

"Same with his kid."

"A locker for his own kind?"

"He's not one of us." The shortstop's eyes were fixed on the boy, his fists clenched.

The boy cowered and realized he was witness to the last bubbles of the eruption. But he understood the venom would continue to spew, to drip, to move insatiably, in an invisible lahar, a slurry of bile, smoking pus and rancid chunks of human hate would continue to move toward his father and him.

"Is he sub-human too?" With that, the tall player got up off the ground and looked over at the Wiffle ball practice.

"He's old. No way that guy is a ballplayer."

"Separate but equal—would that be OK?" He gestured toward right field.

Standing now behind his dad, the boy turned away, bent over, and for no apparent reason and without warning, threw up.

"I say, if he's gonna be here, he needs to keep his kid away from us."

"Stop!" With that, the tall man started to walk toward right field, shaking his hand like someone trying to flick mud off.

The shortstop continued on as the tall man walked away. "We're real pro ball players. If he comes near me, I'll take him out."

The tall man ignored his friend continuing to walk away and too himself said. "So why don't you just put up a burning cross in his yard."

PERFECT

A mericans started playing Abner Doubleday's version of baseball in 1839 and in all that time, no man had ever hit more home runs in a row, or in more consecutive games, than this most improbable little man who, nine weeks ago, was working anonymously behind an old beat-up desk in a tool and die factory.

Tonight, he was placed in one of the most emotionally challenging situations that a hitter can face. Tonight, he was called on to bat in a 0–0 game with two outs in the ninth to face a surefire Hall of Fame pitcher in what might possibly be this Hall of Famer's very last appearance.

Usually, that would be more than enough, but tonight was an extraordinary night because he was being asked to break up that same Hall of Famer's attempt to pitch a perfect game. Asked to do all that while he continued in the pursuit of perfection, seeking a ninth consecutive hit, and a ninth straight home run. Every person in the stadium stopped what they were doing, each aware of the significance of this at bat, and rose to their feet as he entered the batter's box. They all knew that right now, both these men were perfect. In just a few minutes, only one would be.

The last time he batted, it took twenty-four pitches before he finally hit a home run. On this night, against a pitcher who had not given up a single hard-hit ball all night, it took just one pitch. Tonight, his name will be recorded for all time in the annals of baseball history. Batting with a broken hand, he swung at the first pitch and hit a towering home run deep into the left-field seats to end the game.

But after the game, nobody was talking about that. As shocking as the ending of that fantastic game was, the most electrifying moment of the night came after. When all everybody wanted to talk about was the mesmerizing pitching performance or the stunning, game-winning, record-setting home run, the dad dropped a bomb during the press conference by casually announcing his immediate retirement from baseball.

NIGHT

By this time of night, only a few people remained in the stadium, all of them busy completing tasks. The scramble of press wanting interviews went on forever, and a few friends from home waited around to say hi and visit a bit. The loud neighbor wanted the dad to sign "a few balls," and so he signed them. He felt foolish doing it, but why not?

The longest part was saying goodbye to all his teammates and staff that he had actually become friends with. Nine weeks earlier, when he walked into the locker room, not a single one said hello. Tonight, all except one said goodbye.

The paycheck fairy came again, wouldn't want to miss that. Through it all, for over two hours, the boy waited for him to come and play.

By the time he was able to break away, the field was dark, lit only by a few distant maintenance lights that threw as many shadows as they did light, but it was enough for the dad and boy. They didn't bother setting up all the "stuff." They just played the game, and it was fun. The boy won the first two games 5–1 and 4–1, but by the last inning of the third game, the dad finally hit a few home runs and was leading going into the boy's last at bat.

As was his way, the boy had been shuffling through his collection of batting stances all night. When he walked up to bat in the last inning, he got in a brand-new batting stance. He bent his knees and pushed them way apart, and kept his elbows so close together they almost touched. Then he leaned back toward the umpire a bit and tilted his bat away from the pitcher like Rod Carew used to do. The dad went weak kneed when he realized who the boy was doing—him.

Just then, someone somewhere turned off those last couple of lights. Too dark to play but not wanting to go, they sat down on the field to talk. They would often sit together, and the dad would talk to the boy, tell him things, things about his family, the world, any topic really. The dad imagined that the boy liked to hear him talk, although he wasn't sure. More than anything, the dad wished he could actually have conversations with his son, like dads and sons do, like friends do. He wanted to hear what the boy was thinking, to learn about his day, or find out if he liked sitting with his dad at Comerica Park in the middle of the night. Anything, really.

The dad felt guilty about taking the boy from his home and away from all he knew. He told the boy that, in the morning, they would be going home, and looked for any indication that the boy had feelings about that news. He had no way of knowing the boy's thoughts about it, if this was good or not, so they sat together as friends often do, the dad watching passing planes, and the boy picking blades of grass.

In the darkness, he was suddenly aware of the boy looking at him. They held each other's gazes for several seconds, and then he heard his boy's soft voice for the first time as he said: "Thanks, Dad. This has been great!"

SUNDAY MORNING

Morning's heavenly light poured its misty fingers across the dad's face, flooding through the yard's big oaks. Fall had come early this year, and a thick dusting of frost coated the carpet of freshly fallen leaves in his yard. He closed his eyes and listened to the rhythm of his breathing, taking time to think about absolutely nothing but the peace and quiet and the perfection of the morning.

The drive home last night took about an hour, and they arrived quite late. The mom had the car packed so they could leave immediately after the game, but then the press conference happened, then Wiffle ball, and they ended up not leaving Detroit until almost 2 a.m. But now he was home, finally home again. It was 7 a.m., and he wanted time alone before the rest of the house woke up. He leaned against the Jacuzzi with his cup of coffee, inhaling the smell of a fresh frost, trying to wrap his mind around all that had happened and what it meant to be home. Soaking up the morning sun on his face, he marveled as diamonds of light formed by melting frost hung as dew from twigs offered by the oaks.

He had a big day planned, and the most important thing on the list was to visit his boss in the hospital. After that, he was hoping to sneak into work to get a feel for the place before he started again on Monday. But most of all, he just wanted to be back in his home and have a chance to settle in.

Chilled by a new breeze, he moved inside and looked out at his world. Soon, the sun had done its job and melted all that beautiful frost to uncover a barren scape scarred by clumps of wet brown leaves. The yard looked smaller now and not as pure as memory would have it. Things were off; things needed attention. The door on the shed had slipped, shingles were torn, a few boards were loose along the fence, and inexplicably, the family had been joined by a population of moles who had happily been building trails under the untended yard.

Since he was hypnotized by Major League commitments, trips home seemed pointless. The family had assumed a quick departure, so an extra trip seemed extraneous, but one thing led to another, and pretty soon, it had been nine weeks since they had seen home. When they got the call, they dropped everything to be guests of the Tigers. It was an invitation, an unexpected prize, earned for Minor League heroics, and it never occurred to them they would not be back that same day.

The home was frozen in time exactly how they left it. There was a sink full of dirty dishes left soaking, the water long since evaporated, as had the milk in the boy's half-eaten bowl of Cheerios, and all the potted house plants had withered. The dad started a fresh sink, and as the water filled, he looked around the house. A fine layer of dust covered everything, and some rather impressive cobwebs had appeared in the corners. The bread on the shelf in front of him had progressed through many stages of mold, and the plants had given up their petals to the carpet below where the vacuum cleaner waited, still mid-path as it was when the phone rang ten weeks ago.

The neighbor had been mowing the lawn and fetching the mail, and the dad was staring at a big pile of it neatly placed on the kitchen table, waiting for his attention. It occurred to him that this is the first time in his life he did not dread opening the mail for fear of not being able to pay a bill. Unseen, his wife came up behind him and hugged him, a position they silently held for several long seconds. Finally inspired by the postal pile, she broke the mood. "We've been pretty spoiled for the last however long that was, but it looks like we got some work to do around here. Don't ya think?"

"Ya, but I need to do something first, OK?"

The trip to see the boss was very emotional for him. Apparently, the boss had been having mini strokes for longer than anyone realized, and all the crazy phone calls, the inability to follow directions, and his nonsensical solutions were just symptoms. He had been trapped in an altered reality since soon after the dad left. When the big stroke finally hit, it left his friend paralyzed, unable to move his left side, his arm and leg rendered still. Mentally he remained chained in to a reality other than the present, and while happy enough, he was clearly no longer the same man, and this new man no longer recognized the dad.

When the dad arrived, there was no time to visit. Extended family had decided to move his boss, his friend, to a location closer to where they lived, and the dad happened to arrive just as that was happening. So, he watched as they loaded his friend on the ambulance that would take him to a nursing home in Arizona, near the boss's brother. The dad stood at the hospital entrance, watching that ark drive away, blaming himself for ignoring those symptoms for his own self-centered concerns.

In search of a distraction from self-loathing, he decided to see what surprises work held for him. When he arrived at his daytime home for the last twenty years, the tool crib, the only thing left was his decades-old office desk, and a cardboard box containing all his personal items from the desk.

The entire cage and all its contents were missing, and the only tangible evidence that it ever existed were the dark, unpainted spots on the floor that showed where the rows of heavy metal shelving used to stand. He sat in the dim light looking at the missing memories of his last two decades, trying to wrap his mind around the meaning of it. In the distance, the sharp click of dress shoes made their way up the hall. A young man appeared and, smiling, moved toward him with an outstretched hand.

The mom had spent the day fixing up the house all shiny and clean the way she liked it. She bought some new house plants, some bread, and hired a service to clean up the yard; then, together, they sat at the kitchen table, and she listened to his day.

He tried to act excited and told her about the smart young man, who was his new boss. Of how he completely changed everything and put computers and scan codes everywhere. That the tool crib was gone and that his job didn't exist anymore. That the boss was excited to give him a raise, a promotion, and make him a salesman. He thought they could take advantage of his baseball career, to use him to drum up new business and talk with old customers. "People want to hear baseball stories, tell them what the major leagues were like!" And they wanted him to wear a suit, tie, and dress shoes from now on.

When he finished, there was a long silence as they absorbed the ramifications. She took a sip of coffee, then placed the cup perfectly on the coaster, looked at him for a few seconds, and said: "Well, you adapted pretty well last time you changed jobs, so maybe this will be fun for you."

"Maybe? I don't know what else to do. I don't have any other skills, do I?"

After another long pause and another sip of coffee, he said: "Gotta buy a suit, I guess."

"Ya, and some shoes!"

They watched the boy outside the window, flapping as a breeze blew through the yard. When it faded, the dad went on: "I wanted to come home. Don't know what I was expecting, but it's different, it doesn't fit the same."

The knock at the door was the neighbor, but the man that entered was much calmer than the dad remembered. They started with normal chitchat about nothing before he finally offered:

"Want ya to know, there was this couple, knocked on my door an hour or so ago asking if I knew where you lived. Been a lot of crazies snooping around your house since you were gone, so I sent them on a wild goose chase. Might come back, though.

The first group to have kids with them, two little girls, twins I think, said they knew you. They gave me a phone number for ya." He handed them a piece of paper.

"Hey, listen, I gotta run. Let's talk some time once you get settled back in, K?"

"Wait, wait, we have something to give you, for helping out while we were gone—wait here one sec." The mom quickly disappeared down the hall and returned with a baseball bat. "Honey, sign this, it's not much!"

"No. He doesn't want an old bat!"

"Sure, I do!" said the neighbor, grinning from ear to ear.

"Just sign it!" She handed the dad a Sharpie and held the thick end out for him to autograph.

"Say something nice on it."

"OK, as you can tell, I didn't have the time to wrap it," said the mom apologetically.

"That's fine, this is so cool!"

"He used it to hit one of those home runs—not sure which one, think that last one, but I thought you might like it."

ECHO

A few hours later the family of twins had finally managed to locate and meet up with the family of the boy. It had been less than a day since they said their goodbyes but the moms were excited to see each other again and acted like long lost sisters at first sight. The house quickly became a study in Rockwellian stereotypes with the ladies happily talking and making a far too large dinner in the kitchen. The kids escaped to the backyard where they played happily oblivious to the purpose of the visit. Meanwhile the men sprawled motionless in easy chairs intently watching an unimportant baseball game on the TV.

Before long, the grown-ups gathered at the kitchen table, and the associate GM's for the Detroit Tigers offered the dad a deal. "So those are the details, and that is our offer. Do you understand what we are trying to do and what we need from you?" The dad gave a happy nod in the affirmative, and then there was a long pause as the mom and dad looked at each other, smiling.

Looking at their happy faces, the associate manager realized he had forgotten to cover the business topics, so he went on, "You have an exceptional Major League resume now, so we would like to offer you six thousand dollars a day as compensation. You'll get paid for every day that you are on the team; we can guarantee a place on the team for the remainder of the season—that's twenty-one days. We would also like to offer you a signing bonus of one hundred thousand dollars.

"If you come back, during that time, you can have the

apartment to use again for the rest of the season. Our plan is to use you like a pinch hitter, but more than that, we want you to help the young guys we're gonna call up get acclimated, as a kind of ambassador. We hope you can get one more at bat on the last day so we can advertise the heck out of it and make our money back. And there is probably also some publicity and some interviews you'll have to do. I'm betting that could be substantial. After that, next season we'll do the same thing, until you finally become mortal and quit hitting home runs. Then, we'll make you a full-time ambassador and you can work in sales, promotions, and special events doing PR for the team."

There was a long pause as they all looked around at each other, then, the mom, the mother of twins, and the associate GM of the Detroit Tigers all simultaneously said: "So what do you think? Wanna give it a try?"

The GM pushed the contract across the table at the dad. "You will be on the clock as soon as you sign the contract."

The dad looked up at the man who was offering him a plate of gold, then instantly leaned in and signed the contract as the two wives hugged each other and giggled.

FINAL AT BAT

When a team "gives up the ghost" or starts to "play out the string," it means they have stopped trying. Giving up the ghost means something has stopped working, and when a team has lost all chances of winning a championship, they will often play out the string. The expression comes from football. Strings are the lineups, and there are first, second, third, and fourth string players. The first string are the best players, the starters, second string are the backups, and the third and fourth string players are those remaining on the team who seldom play. When a team play out the string, it has made a choice to no longer worry about competing and play all its players, including the least among them.

Today was the last game of the season, and both teams had given up the ghost and were playing out the string. Both lineups were full of young Minor League prospects called up in September to get a look and a taste of baseball at the Major League level during the last weeks of the season.

During the golden age of sailing, understanding how to tie knots and handle the ropes were essential skills expected of sailors at every level. Experienced sailors would teach the newer ones the ropes, knots, the tricks of the trade to make sure that when their time came, they could do their job for the good of all. Knowledge was passed on by sailors with experience to those without with the understanding that the ship sailed smoother if all sailors knew the ropes. The dad had become the baseball equivalent of the old sailors making it a point to teach the new arrivals to the major leagues all the little details a player needed to thrive. It had not occurred to the dad, but he had grown in many ways since his days of hiding in a dark tool crib all day. He'd turned into a gracious, jovial, confident man who enjoyed the company of his fellow man and meeting new people.

While the dad did not really know the catcher from his Minor League team, he was nonetheless excited to see him. The dad made a point of taking him around and introducing him personally to every Major League player in the locker room. And not just a "hi, how are ya" greeting either—each introduction left the new player feeling comfortable and like he knew the man he had just met. The dad introduced him not only to players but to the old man who mowed the lawns, the trainers, the security guards, and the vendor who snuck him a few hot dogs during every game. The dad had made it his job to take each new player and show him the ropes, to make him part of the team.

Without realizing it, the dad had also become an ambassador for the game since he announced his immediate retirement two weeks ago, and he was playing the role in earnest. He had fully intended to walk away to a happy retirement in his backyard and his old life. Yet, as is the way with baseball money, he found himself still with the team because they begged him to finish out the season for a $100,000 bonus. Begging that loudly can break the will of even the most disinterested soul.

As they played out the string, teams had suddenly started treating him as if he were baseball royalty. While the dad was uncomfortable with the big fuss some of the teams had been making with his retirement, he had long since learned to not tilt at the windmills of instincts that told him to avoid the spotlight. Each team had a pregame ceremony and made a big fuss over his accomplishments. He had been universally showered with gifts in each city, as if he were a beloved native son who had played the game for twenty years. One team gave him a rocking chair, the next a golf cart, and the third gave him a fantastic bass boat, as they seemed to compete to give him bigger and better going away gifts. It all seemed rather absurd to him, but he smiled graciously. Today was the last day of the season, so like it or not, this was the end. Now on his last day, the team had asked him to bat one final time. Figuring he had nothing left to prove, he agreed.

With all that had happened, it was only fitting that it would end how it began. It was inevitable that there would be another first time during one of his at bats. This was the first time he would bat against a man for the second time. He faced this goliath of a man in an at bat that people are still talking about. Little did they know that the at bat that was about to happen would never be forgotten.

Surely, bygones would be bygones, and the mood seven weeks ago would be different—nothing was riding on this game. Everyone knew that this at bat was ceremonial, a send-off, just a going-away present of sorts. Still, he couldn't help but shudder a bit as he stood there in the on-deck circle as they changed pitchers, and he watched this monster warming up. The giant did not have the same menace about him. He was different now. He seemed possessed by a calmer, more determined quality than before, the dad thought as he studied him.

For his part, the dad was no longer fearful. He knew his fate, and had already proven himself in the eyes of baseball history, and more importantly, to himself. He had shown that he belonged without question. Of all his accomplishments, the dad took the greatest pride not in all the home runs, but in that he had a perfect batting average. "Oh well," he thought as the last warm-up pitch was thrown, "all things come to an end."

Finally, the old umpire yelled, "Play ball." The dad walked calmly into the batter's box and set himself for the pitch, then looked over at his son one last time. The pitcher oddly tipped his hat toward the dad's dugout, then immediately went into his windup and released the ball. The dad's batting average would remain a perfect; perfect on this day, perfect forever.

The sound of the ball hitting made a loud crack, and the

ball rolled hard and fast until it finally settled in and came to a stop in shallow center field. No one bothered to field it, but every player allowed it to stop on its own. With the sound of the ball hitting its target, almost every infielder immediately started a slow jog toward home plate, as did every player in each dugout.

The dad's friend, the Minor League catcher, was the first to reach him, but the training staff sprinted toward home plate and moved him out of the way as the stadium went dead silent.

When the trainers reached the dad, he was in a heap on home plate. His helmet had flown off, and once again, his glasses lay in pieces on the ground. The 98 mph fastball had hit him flush on the nose, caving in the front of his face and sending a thousand fragments of broken cartilage and bone shooting into his head. The dad lay at home plate, perfectly still.

The trainers were frantic as players instinctively circled them in efforts to form a wall around this gruesome visage, shielding cameras, the stands, and most of all, his son from the awful view. The strongest men among them struggled to hold back tears as they watched the heroic efforts of the medical staff. The only noise in the stadium were the sounds of CPR, of grunts, counting, snapping ribs, and the low sobs of the boy's mom in the stands as she held the boy tightly to her chest, surrounded by whispers of disbelief among the sinners in the crowd.

But there was nothing to be done, until at last, one by one, the trainers stood in sad defeat. The circle of players grew tighter and tighter around him, blocking out the light, until only a few fragments of light fell upon his shattered face.

FOG

At first, the fog, as if an ember glowed, a cruel dull jaundice ache struggling to find form. Betrayed by them no longer, he began to trust the comprehension of his senses, aware of a building brightness within the soupy broth surrounding him. Yellow, the view in all directions was a flat, clean, even wash of uninterrupted yellow, like fog, only yellow. It was thick, a syrup so dense the dad could not see finger or form or hands, arms, or any part of the body when he looked for them, all gone, blotted by a fog, blood like in thickness. Like a firefly, the mist's vapors glowed internally. No external illuminations acted upon it. This world had an illogical, ethereal quality about it, him a mere mite, disoriented, irrelevant, and misplaced within it.

Very far away, a tiny thing appeared; a black speck, fixed at first, it began to vibrate. As he watched, the thing started to flip back and forth spastically, like a flea on a hot surface. He observed the curious object, wondering about its purpose, and soon perceived it had started to spin, slow at first, the pace increasing over time. The random peculiarities of this shifting shape tested his powers of concentration, and as he watched a dread told him to fear this black speck, and so he did. He resolved it best to ignore this beast, to look away, to find other landmarks to ponder. He searched in all directions for a moment of contrast, but all vistas were the same wall of ever-thickening yellow syrup, the only beacon visible the odd black speck. Resigned to this fate, he watched it float and bobble like a gnat in front of his eyes until he fell asleep.

Suddenly the profound silence of slumber gave way to low snapping buzz of noise from far beyond that unseen horizon. Puzzled, he tried to place the sound and likened it to the noise of hot grease, full of spits, bubbles, and bursts. He studied the crackling, hoping for clues, but details from the static were beyond his grasp.

Inexplicably, the smell of bacon overwhelmed him. "Was someone near, were they cooking?" But, the sudden smell of bacon morphed and became a kaleidoscope of aromas, putrid, then acrid, and on to ether and ammonia. Harsh, uncomfortable, they burned his eyes, releasing salty tears, so he shut them tightly. In this new darkness, he was aware of new and distant noises. Did he hear the cadence of someone speaking? Not the sound or content of speaking but the rhythm of it, like whispers, only it was not whispering. "What was that?" he thought. No, not whispers, but like the hum of bees, heard through many layers of walls. Then it would spike like a single voice was trying to call to him.

His eyes, the wrong organ, opened and tried to locate the sounds through the rancid yellow mist but echoes from all directions provided only lies, giving no satisfaction to his search. His vision useless, a lost utility further confusing where the fog ended and his skin began, so he tried to move, his feet reached out, fawn-like, first steps awkward, searching to find ground, unable to locate solid footing. He realized he was adrift, floating in a sea of eternal sands that gave way to his every wave and gesture, offering no resistance that could lead to propulsion. Perplexed, his arms and legs were now just useless tubes of meat, flailing randomly to no effect. They no longer made sense to him, odd phantoms, at once connected and at once a mile away, disjointed in another time and place.

The black orb cried out at him again as if to say "notice me," spinning faster. Now the perfection of its spin began to wobble as if caught in some swirling scape that called to him. He recognized that his fear had vanished, and the speck's hypnotic pulse captivated him, like ball lightning fluttering across the horizon, skittering like water in hot grease. Insatiable now and moving like a moth to a flame, he was somehow moving counter to the vortex. He was conscious of his captured state, and that the fog had formed thick, pudding-like fingers that held him firmly as they too were caught in the twisting storm.

He was moving inexplicably downward, head first, toward that curious black star. Then, there was a depth, and the dot stretched into an inky abyss, cold, a foreboding cold made him feel brittle in the depths, and he was wet, wet, and frozen, and he realized something was wrong for the first time. This was a funnel, he was floating in a cyclonic void, toward a dark, collapsing, unseen tube.

The black spot grew vast as he approached it, it, blending quickly to become a thick a black curtain of darkness now hovering in front of him before, ultimately, total blackness consumed him. All remaining yellow drained away, leaving him floating in perfect darkness. Within this void, he began to feel the breath of unimaginable wings and staccato gusts of powerful winds, moving him through the void, ice-cold bursts ripping at his flesh. He found comfort in the power and rhythm of these breaths, and helpless, drifted off to the edge of sleep.

Terror woke his complacency when he realized the wings were gone and no longer floating; now, unmistakably, he was falling. He could see nothing, only feel the cold, steady winds cut at him. His speed increased. Terrified, he clawed hopelessly at the foggy fingers, searching to find the sides of the funnel, anything to grab, to break his fall. Sensing an end, screaming now, voiceless, his panic intensified as he felt accelerations of ridiculous speeds.

At the height of his panic was the perplexing awareness he was no longer moving. He was instead inside a tremendous warmth, cocooned by a thickness that enveloped him inside a vast expanse of weightless grit. Just a sludgy resistance held him safe.

Suddenly he felt pressure on his chest, and a great warmth moved through his body, and he was glad for this. There was a rhythm to the weight, and with each pressure, the heat would return, cycling on and off, the passions of cold when it receded. In the distance there was a white dot, at first bringing relief to the darkness that frightened him so. He tried to wave at it, to call it, but the sands held his limbs still.

His curiosity became concern as he puzzled upon this mystery and realized a white dot was growing and advancing toward him very fast. He blinked and struggled to escape as he realized the spinning blur of anger and pain was coming in search of him. He gave one last flex for freedom, but the sands had hardened around him.

A brilliant flash of white filled his vision, and then pain filled his head as the blazing meteor crashed into him, his head exploding as if suddenly consumed by shards of glass. Unsure of what had happened, he was now afraid to move or even breathe. Confused, he held a rigid form, praying the predator was gone.

Something changed as a cool breeze licked across his face. Opening his eyes, he realized his pain was gone and he was somehow standing. Calm now, feeling no fear, urgency, or panic, he felt good, so he took the time to study this new environment.

"What a curiosity was this?" he said, looking around. At his feet was the dirt around home plate, and this was a base-ball field; only everything was white. Beyond the confines of the park, this world was a bright white void. But in the area around him was a baseball field. Not foggy or misty, but like on a bright clear day, all of it was white. The grass was white, the dirt, all details found in a baseball field various shades of bright white, save one oddity that concerned him now.

Out by the far edge of center field was that little black speck. He studied it, and as he did, it took form and became a dark shape. Within it, he could see billowing black clouds that bubbled and twisted, shifting into patterns until he realized it had become a man, and that man was looking directly at him. The dad looked down at himself. Then, touching and patting to confirm his limbs were working again, he listened to an inner voice that urged him to talk with this man. The man was standing, looking directly at him in a fixed, unblinking gaze. He began to walk toward the man, and as he neared him, he studied the man's features and felt a curious familiarity that he did not understand.

Before him was a strong young man of athletic build, immaculate professional dress, clearly a man articulate in the ways of modern society, handsome with a chiseled jaw, clean-shaven, and a thick, close-cut crop of jet-black hair. He looked familiar, and they studied each other as the man's cerulean eyes remained fixed on him. The dad stopped in front of him, and the man greeted him with a perfect smile and a firm handshake.

The dad blinked, and when his eyes opened, the man had aged, his hair now grayed, his face lined, and his jaw sagged a bit. Disoriented at the sudden passage of time, the dad spoke: "Do I know you?"

"You do!" said the man, smiling back at him.

There was a long pause as the two men studied each other. The dad blinked, and again the man's age had changed; this time, the younger one stood before him once again.

"How are you, Dad?" said the young man, smiling warmly.

The dad was stunned and took a few seconds to absorb the man who stood before him. Too shocked to speak, all he could muster was a whispered: "Chad?"

"Yes, this is one version of me," said Chad, continuing the direct stare and bright smile.

"I don't understand."

Chad knew what he meant and without being asked offered, "This is the way you wished I were."

"I'm confused."

Understanding and nodding in agreement, Chad said, "That's OK. This is big. Who wouldn't be?" He then gave his dad time to catch his breath a bit before finally moving on. "We don't have much time, Dad."

"Why?" said the dad, looking around as if a new oddity would appear to sweep him away.

"This place is just a holding place."

"Holding place?"

"It's a place we can be, so you don't hurt while we do this" Chad explained.

"Do what? Hurt? Is it bad?"

"Talk, and yes, it's horrible."

"Will I get better?"

Chad paused a long time to allow his dad to process the ramifications of his questions before moving on with the discussion.

"We haven't decided yet." Again, Chad allowed for a long space between words here to enable these concepts to bubble in his father's brain. "Do you want to get better?"

The dad realized that this was a once-in-a-lifetime question, that there was no bigger question to be answered. "I think so." The dad looked away and considered where he was and all the things he had just experienced. "So, all this, it's not real?"

"It's not. It's an in-between place."

"But why?"

"Think of it like a calm, or a pause, before the hurt starts, or the other thing happens."

The dad looked back at Chad again. "The other thing?" Chad just nodded his head slightly.

"Does the pain have to come back? Do I?" said the dad.

"Well, those are the two paths, the two questions."

Wanting to take a break from the intensity of the topic, the dad changed the subject. "I got hit?"

"Yes." After another long break to think, he circled back now. "Dad, this is a place that allows us to talk. Here, we can speak, father and son. I can talk while we are here, and you can hear me, here, in this place, for at least for a few minutes."

Realizing the enormity of his next words, the dad again took a moment to think. Finally, he went on. "Oh, there is so much to say, to ask. I've thought about this—what to say, lots of times, but now, I don't know."

"Yes, you do. Ask."

The father thought about it, looked at the dirt, kicked it

with his toe, and then looked back up at the boy.

"Are you happy? I mean out there?"

"I am . . . extremely happy."

"You are?"

"I am, I could not ask for a better life."

"Really?"

"I know there is no way for you to tell, but I hear and see everything. I understand everything, more than you! And yes, I am thrilled. You and Mom are great parents, and I would not change a thing."

"Will you grow up to be this?"

"No, this is for now—for here, this one time, I will always be what I am, which is very happy—as long as you go back."

"Do I have to?"

The two men looked at each other until Chad raised his eyebrows and said, "It's up to you, but Mom needs you. I do too."

Then, after one last pause before the final chorus:

"Will I remember this?"

"No, but you will feel it."

"Are you ready?"

"Yes."

Suddenly in darkness, he was moving fast again, pulled through the thick pudding sands, jerking left and right and head over heels. Intense pain stabbed his head from every direction, and a pounding filled the spots in between.

He opened his eyes, and once again, all he could see was white, but this was different. He could hear the muffled sounds of people speaking and sensed the presence of still others closer to him. Through the whiteness, he discerned the silhouettes of large creatures towering over him. They looked down at him, as if deciding his fate, as if he were in the presence of gods. Searing pain torched his every nerve beyond comprehension; it ate at him and left him frozen at the fear of it and them.

Within it all, he felt the lightest touch, and with it, a blast like thunder rolled through his head. Clouds of pain started to slowly drift away until, at last, just a dull ache was all that remained.

He coughed hard and sat up fast, continuing to hack. He realized he had a sheet over his head and swatted at it to untangle himself. When it cleared, he looked around and saw Chad kneeling next to him, now ten years old again. Behind him was the mom holding his shoulders, and all around them were the members of the team.

FIRST PITCH

When the dad arrived for the game, there was a forty-eight-foot semi "Kentucky" moving truck in the parking lot that was hogging all the good parking spots right by the front entrance to the ball field. It had been five years since the movers first cooked for the mom and the mother of twins. Since then, the Moving Company had become a wildly successful regional restaurant chain with five-star dining in the back of a spectacularly designed tractor-trailer truck. It featured fantastic food offered in a different location every night.

Today, though, they were selling their food at a baseball game. This came to be because the ladies realized that the men had fantastic cooking and decorating skills, and believed there was more potential for those talents than in moving people's goods from point A to point B. In the end, the men used those skills to design an amazingly beautiful mobile restaurant specializing in location-specific dining and incredible food. The trailer part of the truck became an expanding luxury dining area for twenty tables with floor to ceiling sliding glass doors designed to allow patrons to enjoy the great outdoors, an event, or game as if on a covered patio, all while eating high-end cooking.

High schools had even started hiring six or seven trucks at a time to host proms. The semitrucks would circle wagon-train style in a high school parking lot. They would put down a temporary dance floor in the middle, string some lights between the trucks, put the band in the middle, and hocus pocus

—prom in the round. It was a win-win solution for everybody. High school principals and parents loved it because they had total control of the campus and didn't need to worry about long drives, hotel rooms, or outsiders on their campus. And the owners loved it because they got to cook for four hundred kids and their dates.

The dad made a point to pass through the diner's platform on the way into the field. Baseball fans liked it when he stopped to shake hands and tell stories with folks while they dined. He was visiting at a table, and his wife walked by and swatted him on the butt.

"I didn't know you were working this one," said the dad. "Yep, just until the game starts. One of our waitresses called in sick, so owners do whatever is needed, right?"

Just then, the mother of twins passed by, followed her girls, "Hey, you two, nice to see you, honey," she said, walking behind them on her way to greet some late arrivals.

They were all now part of an ownership group who together owned and operated fifteen The Moving Company

The three young men jumped at the proposal, but the supervisor decided he was too old, so he took his cut and retired. Mostly, though, he hung out and supervised whatever was going on and was every bit as involved as always.

"Where is the pops tonight?" the dad asked the mother of twins as she passed by again.

"Oh, he's out behind the backstop cooking burgers; we've got competition tonight," she said, smiling.

Pregame, there was a buzz of anticipation among both teams that day. Sure, they were going to play a game, but the excitement was that players on both sides had heard rumors who was going to be in attendance to watch, and the rumor was that there would be a Major League presence.

While over time the boy joined the world of speakers, he had never developed the gift of gab or even extended conversation. This deficit ensured that, at this point in his life, he did not have close friends. In spite of that, he was one of the more popular kids in school; in many ways, of course, it was the legend of his father that made his inclusion possible. Five years ago, the dad spent nine weeks playing Major League Baseball, and the fables of his exploits made the boy's presence at high school events mandatory. But, while his father's fame got him included the first time, the other kids realized that, beyond pedigree, he was a friendly kid and was fun to have around, so they invited him back again.

For the last five years, the boy had continued to spend his summers throwing Wiffle ball batting practice to the Detroit Tigers while his dad worked doing special projects for the team. The boy became a team mascot to players, and over time a few pitchers taught him how to throw a real baseball. Now, five years later, the boy was a tall, handsome, athletic sixteen year old

The high school coach early on decided that if it was good enough for the Detroit Tigers, it must be good enough for his high school team, so he invited the boy to throw batting practice to his team as well. Quickly the high school coach saw what the MLB pitchers had been teaching Chad and that the boy had some skills beyond Wiffle ball. Once his ability was proven, the boy quickly moved up, and today was going to be his first time starting an actual game.

The dad could not have been prouder of his boy and, of course, told his friends, who all showed up for the game. His friends just happened to be MLB players. So, in addition to the regular audience that attended high school baseball games when teams with 4–7 records play, the crowd also included two MLB all-stars, a pair of old MLB coaches, and seven or eight other MLB players.

When the dad finally made it to the field, the grounds crew of the Detroit Tigers was putting the finishing touches on the high school field. Meanwhile, all his friends and their wives were standing around the barbeque grill, watching the old mover cook hamburgers. The jovial group was visiting with fans and signing autographs, telling stories, and making fun of the newly named all-stars.

One of those new all-stars was the left fielder who had been destroying curveballs for the past five years. The other was the catcher the dad met in the minor leagues, bonded forever in baseball history in the image, akin to Kent State, of him kneeling in horror next to the dad the day he died at home plate.

In spite of being given up for dead, the dad was doing quite well, thank you very much. Once the physical injuries had healed, and the pain subsided, there were still symptoms from a ball hitting his face at 100 mph. The doctors were slow to understand the remaining symptoms, but once they did, they all had a great laugh about it. The dad's symptoms were truly bizarre. It turned out he suffered from a rare condition called synesthesia, and he was now a synesthete. A synesthetic is a person who has some or all of their five senses work or respond in nontraditional ways.

In the dad's case, his five senses had become confused, and his vision, taste, smell, and touch got turned all catawampus. Since the beaning, any time the dad saw the color yellow, it made him smell bacon. Conversely, seeing actual bacon made him hear wind noises and taste chocolate. Ironically, while real bacon tasted like bacon, tasting actual chocolate gave him vertigo, or made him feel like he is floating. Large white areas or fog provoked a phantom feeling of sand rubbing on his skin. And, at all times, he could see glowing colors around people. The odd part was that there appeared to be no rhyme or reason for why, how, or when these colors would appear. The one exception was that the boy almost always had a bright yellow fuzz that would outline or follow him, and the boy, therefore, smelled like bacon all the time.

The game was about to start, and the boy walked out to the mound to take his warm-up pitches. Realizing the significance of the moment, they all stopped their visits at the barbeque to watch the boy. Seven warm-up pitches later, the umpire yelled, "Play ball!" and everyone grew quiet and drifted toward the fence.

The dad and his wife stood there holding hands, noses pressed against the chain-link fence. The sudden realization struck the dad that his boy was about participate in something official for the first time in his life. Spontaneously the dad's eyes filled with tears as the boy leaned in to look at the catcher for the sign. Then, standing tall for the first pitch, he turned his head, stared directly at the dad, and smiled. Through watery eyes, the dad saw the face of the handsome man smiling at him and began to silently sob when he felt his wife squeeze his hand. Mercifully, the boy looked away and went into his windup as someone attached to the hands on the dad's shoulder whispered, "Nice job, you two!"

AFTERWORD

Later, as he relaxed in the glorious Michigan sunshine, the dad shut his eyes and allowed the dancing black dot to hypnotize him the way he had become accustomed to. Over time, this crazy speck had become a source of comfort and relaxation for him. No matter his mood or situation, he could always shut his eyes, and inexplicably this strange little autokinetic visitor would kick in to keep him entertained and cheer him up. During this moment of luxury, he made plans to watch Chad and the twins try some vertical jigging in the boat Chad inherited from the groundskeeper. After that, maybe they would try to ride some horses with the moms.

Feeling guilty about what had become for him a guilty pleasure, his eyes blinked open, the dancing dot replaced with the image of Chad chasing a Wiffle ball. Chad still liked to wear that old jersey while he played Wiffle ball, and it was clear the boy loved this new world. The oversize Adirondack chair allowed the dad room to blissfully sprawl on the pool deck, sipping a beer and watching a blur of colors follow Chad as he played Wiffle ball with the twins, the two moms, and a couple of his high school teammates.

The dad's mind drifted to what incomprehensible cosmic connections must have occurred for him and his family for things to turn out this way. For the first twenty years of his life, he was a lost soul searching for purpose in a world full of lost souls. He spent the next twenty years hiding from his self-imposed shame as punishment that he never found a meaning to his life. He served his sentence double padlocked in a claustrophobic jail cell/tool crib, using the excuse that it was work as justification for the punishment. At home, he hid with his boy, locked away from the world inside the tall planks of the backyard fence; even their Wiffle ball game carefully protected him from intrusion from the outside world.

All those years he'd wasted, not realizing the meaning he was searching for was happily sitting at the dinner table with him. The physical trappings of his life had changed tremendously in the last five years, and his family was lucky enough to have many new things. The pool with the built-in Jacuzzi, the deck, even his Adirondack chairs were symbolic of physical and financial success.

But he now realized all those physical glories were trivial because the most significant changes were the mental ones. Just as tearing down the backyard fence opened them up to see the world, so too was the mental jail gone, and the presence of psychological insecurities that had trapped them for so long. He had seen the edge of the world, and he had brought back souvenirs: personal confidence, social acceptance, a zest for new experiences, and the possibility of a life well lived. Now he looked forward to whatever vision and opportunities the world held for his family.

www.ingramcontent.com/pod-product-compliance
Lightning Source LLC
Chambersburg PA
CBHW020404210626
46816CB00006BB/2115